15.

Site Q:
The Lost City

By

Robert Bresloff

Site Q The Lost City

Pumpkinhead Productions
Email-wanderland@comcast.net

Author's note: Regarding the names used for Mayan cities/ruins, I have used the modern name in all cases so not to confuse the reader.

CHAPTER ONE
The Call

The old man had awakened suddenly. Was it a dream? He glanced at the window to see the light of the full moon as it poured into his small but tidy hut. He slept on the floor just as his ancestors had for over a thousand years. Was it a vision? His mind turned back to the strange images that came to disturb his rest.

The years had been kind to him, he thought as he sat up. The old man thanked the gods that at his age he could still move around without pain or effort. Now fully awake, he moved from his mat and stood. Again, the old man thanked the gods. Picking up a long stick, he poked at the smoldering wood in his fire pot. It took a few minutes, but the embers began to glow. Soon the old man felt the gentle warmth of his fire as it covered his wrinkled face and hands.

Pulling on his coat, he walked outside to fetch wood for the hungry fire. As he stood before his hut, the moon bathed him in a shimmering pale blue light. It was very bright on this night. He stopped and just stared at the mysterious disc that hung so gently in the sky. He wondered what his ancestors felt a thousand years before when they viewed this miracle in the sky. The old man stared up into the heavens. It was difficult to resist thinking what had awakened him on this night was more than a dream. He had no doubt that there was a reason for this vision. He thought of how odd it was. The woman, the island, what did it all mean?

He decided it best to sit down in the night air and let the light of the moon guide his varied thoughts. Remembering this vision was not a problem. Now deeply etched in his memory, it was very real—much too real. What could it mean? He decided to replay the images in his mind So many times he thought about the vision, but found no answer. One thing he did know was that some day he would meet the *one*. The one who would help him understand what had invaded his thoughts. The thoughts that would, undoubtedly, haunt him until he met the *one*.

The summer was hot—about as hot as Woodson could ever remember. He had spent so many years in the Yucatan Peninsula that he had forgotten how darn hot Chicago summers could get.

Built like a fireplug, his face was narrow with strong deep features that ended at a handsome square jaw. A well-known archeologist, Richard Woodson was an expert in ancient Mayan culture, including the mysterious ruins that the Maya had left behind. Woodson sat on the patio looking out over the mirrored lake. He thought of how he longed to return to Mexico. He missed Pedro and Angel and the wonderful sights and smells of the Caribbean.

Woodson was currently on a leave of absence from his archeological duties. The University thought it best that he rested after his ordeal at Chichén Itzá. So he and his girlfriend, Marilynn Trotter (whom he called Blue because of her brilliant blue eyes), were back in the Windy City for some rest and relaxation.

"Hey Woody," said Blue, from just inside the patio door. She carried two tall frosty glasses. "Could you get the door? My hands are full." Woodson jumped up to assist her. As he did, he accidentally dropped a string of small green beads.

"Are you still playing with those silly beads?" Blue asked.

"I guess so," he answered, looking into her big blue eyes. "I just can't get Guerrero out of my mind."

"Look, Lyons told me to keep an eye on you. I know what an emotional roller coaster you were on last month, but you've got to let it go!" Blue sat down next to Woodson and placed her hand affectionately on his. He looked at the beads in his hand and then deeply into her eyes.

"I wish I could," he said softly, "but I miss Pedro, Angel, and the professor. If it weren't for them and the mysterious woman that Pedro said helped pull us to safety, the Sacred Cenote would have swallowed us up."

"I know," said Blue thoughtfully. "But that whole mess is over and done with. The Fifth Codex is lost forever and all you have left are those green beads that you found with Guerrero's journal." Blue grew impatient. "Need I remind you that you're supposed to be resting?"

Woodson stood and walked near the grassy shore. The lake appeared as smooth as glass, rare for a usually windy time of year. Standing at the water's edge for a moment, he paused, looked at the beads, and then quickly stuffed them in his pocket before turning around.

"You're right. You're absolutely right," he agreed. "The Codex is gone. Guerrero's journal is in the museum and Aguilar is in jail—" He heard the phone ring.

"I'll get it," shouted Blue. She ran into the house. Moments later, Blue stepped back outside with the phone. "It's for you."

"Who is it?" he asked.

"He said his name was Jon Panzer. Said that it's really important that he speak with you," Blue frowned as she handed him the phone. "Do you know him?"

Woodson shrugged his shoulders and snatched the phone from Blue. "This is Woodson... yes... I'm the one... University? No... yes, I can... tomorrow... yes, I know

Site Q The Lost City

where that is... two o'clock... sure... okay. I will see you then. Goodbye Mr. Panzer." Handing the phone back to Blue, Woodson turned, and without so much as a word, walked back toward the lake.

"Who was that?" Blue inquired impatiently. "Who's Panzer?"

Woodson stood quietly by the water's edge. He did not answer.

"Woody! Who *is* this Panzer guy?" she pressed on, now sounding annoyed. "What does he want?"

Woodson turned back toward Blue and shot her a half smile. "Only the largest collector of Mayan artifacts in North America... It seems that he wants me!"

"Now what would he want with you?" inquired Blue suspiciously.

"I'm not exactly sure, but it sounded like he wants to hire me."

"To do what?"

"Consulting, more than likely," replied Woodson. He skipped a stone across the surface of the lake. "I'll find out tomorrow at two o'clock."

"Look Woody," began Blue, waving an accusing finger, "You promised Lyons that you would take it easy—"

"Relax Blue," Woodson tried to reassure her, picking up another stone to skip across the lake. "I'm just going to talk to the man. He probably wants to ask some questions about Gonzalo Guerrero. I'm sure that's all."

"Well I'm going with you." Blue continued to wave the menacing finger.

"Not this time." Woodson shook his head. "He just wants to see me."

"What the heck?"

"Panzer wants a private meeting," he quickly interrupted. "Even if you did come, I'm sure he'd have you

6

wait in another room. From what I've heard, these collectors are supposed to be quite eccentric.

Blue dropped heavily into one of the chairs, and with both hands pulled her long brown hair away from her tanned face. "I just *know* you're going to get yourself into trouble. I just know it."

Woodson did not answer. He just stared out over the water. The sun was beginning to set and the clouded sky shrouded the lake with many different shades of orange and pink. Woodson watched the sun slowly set making sure to conceal his smile from Blue.

"*The* Mr. Panzer," he said under his breath. "I think *this* is going to be very interesting!"

CHAPTER TWO
The Meeting

It was nearly two o'clock by the time Woodson arrived in Chicago for his meeting. It was another hot afternoon and he was looking forward to cooling off in the building's air-conditioned lobby. After struggling with the revolving door that led to the lobby, Woodson looked for the building directory. Upon finding Mr. Panzer's office number, he casually made his way to the elevator. Just as he stepped in, he heard a woman's voice cry out from across the lobby.

"Hold the elevator!"

Woodson quickly stretched out his arm blocking the closing door. As the door reopened, the woman hastily stepped in.

"Thanks. The elevators in this building are so slow," she gasped, attempting to catch her breath. The doors quickly closed behind her.

"No problem," replied Woodson politely, giving her the usual boyish once over. Quite attractive, she stood about five feet six, had a shapely muscular build topped off by nearly shoulder length, dishwater blond hair. Her deeply chiseled features framed two beautiful, penetrating green eyes. "What floor Miss?" he inquired courteously.

The woman glanced at the lit floor number button on the brushed metal panel. "Looks like we're going to the same floor," she said still gasping for breath.

Woodson smiled then looked up at the ceiling as most people do while riding in an elevator. When it came to a stop, Woodson politely gestured for the woman to go first. As they left the elevator, he and the woman headed in the same direction. "It seems we're going to the same place," he remarked, feeling a bit embarrassed.

"Then you must be Richard Woodson," she replied. Woodson smiled and tipped his brown leather hat. "Great. I'm glad you made it... I'm sorry... I'm Carla... Carla Jameson." Ms. Jamison grabbed Woodson's hand. Her grip was firm. "I'm Jon's... I mean, Mr. Panzer's assistant." She fumbled with the doorknob before the door finally swung open. "Please do come in, Mr. Woodson."

Woodson removed his hat and stepped inside. With dark marble floors and antique brass light fixtures, the lobby resembled a museum. Woodson stood amazed. The lobby was loaded with artifacts, Mayan artifacts. There were incredibly well preserved codex pottery and deadly looking weapons made of stone. There were stelae; limestone panels carved with intricately chiseled Mayan hieroglyphics. Everywhere Woodson looked were large glass cases that held ancient limestone panels. There were at least six of these panels, each one depicting a different event in Mayan history. He was dumbfounded. In all his years in dealing with the ancient Maya, Woodson had never seen a private collection such as this. He stood frozen—awed—as if he were in the presence of royalty.

Mr. Woodson?" Ms. Jameson attempted to get his attention.

By this time, Woodson's nose pressed against one of the glass cases that held these wonderful artifacts. "Yes? I mean... yes, Ms. Jamison?" he answered, as if woken unexpectedly from a pleasant dream.

Ms. Jamison smiled as she opened a door and motioned for him to enter. "Mr. Panzer will see you now."

Woodson stepped through the doorway. Looking around, he spied artifacts more incredible than what he had already seen. Glass cases lined both sides of the long room ending at a large dark oak desk. Behind the desk sat a slightly built older man wearing thick eyeglasses. His head topped by what appeared to be an awful looking hairpiece. The man sprang from his seat and held out both hands warmly.

"Ah yes, Mr. Woodson. *Bash kawa leek?"* Panzer asked in ancient Yucatec.

Woodson eyed the man curiously. *"Mish baa!"* he replied after a moment.

"Excellent! The famous Mr. Woodson does indeed speak the language of the Maya, Ms. Jamison."

Carla Jamison was just behind Woodson. She had not fully entered the room yet. "What in the world was that all about?" she asked, closing the door behind her.

"I greeted Mr. Woodson and asked him 'what was happening,'" replied the smiling Mr. Panzer.

Woodson turned toward Ms. Jamison and explained, "to which I replied, 'Nothing much.' Mr. Panzer, I presume?" he continued, now facing Panzer. "What can I do for you?"

Panzer showed Woodson to a big stuffed black-leather chair. He made himself comfortable by sitting on the corner of the oak desk. "Glad you could make it, sir," Panzer said with obvious excitement.

Woodson continued to look around the office in disbelief. "You have a splendid collection, Mr. Panzer."

"Thank you. Please, call me Jon. I see you've already met Carla."

"Okay, Mr. Panzer... Jon," began Woodson, "let's skip all the niceties. What am I doing here?"

"A man who gets right to the point," Panzer quickly replied. "I like that." The mysterious collector took a deep breath before he spoke, "I need to know what happened to you in the Yucatan. I have heard conflicting reports. Is it true that you actually experienced ancient Mayan occult?"

Woodson suddenly felt uncomfortable. He shifted nervously in the chair. "You get right to the point, yourself,

Mr. Panzer," he replied before relating what had happened in regards to The Fifth Codex.

Woodson told Panzer of how he and his assistant Pedro had found the writings of Gonzalo Guerrero one of the first Spaniards to set foot in the Yucatan. How the shipwrecked Guerrero was taken in by the Maya, and lived the rest of his life with them. Woodson went on to describe Guerrero's journal going into some detail of Guerrero's life with the Maya and his constant references to a mysterious fifth codex. How the criminal, Aguilar, had stolen this codex in his pursuit of immortality, and of how the Maya God L reclaimed the codex for all time in the deep waters of the Sacred Cenote at Chichén Itzá.

When Woodson finished, Panzer stood and walked around his desk. Sitting in another leather chair, this one adorned with small Mayan symbols along the rounded arms, he opened a highly polished wooden cigar box. "Cuban?" He offered Woodson a cigar. "Did Guerrero's journal ever mention the existence of a lost city?" he inquired.

"No thanks..." Woodson motioned toward the cigars and shook his head. "As a matter a fact it did! Why?"

"Have you ever heard of Site Q. in Guatemala?" Panzer answered with another question.

"Sure. Who hasn't? Archeologists know that there is still another great Mayan city waiting in some deep jungle... Except the looters, of course, not only have they found the city; they sell off the artifacts they steal. I would imagine by the look of your collection, Mr. Panzer that you might have a few of those pieces yourself." Woodson did not try to hide the impatience in his voice. Archeologists disdained the fact that collectors like Panzer deprived the public of experiencing great archeological finds. "What does all of this have to do with me?"

"I'll get right to the point," replied Panzer "I'm going to finance an expedition to find Site Q. I want you to lead it, Mr. Woodson."

Woodson just sat there staring at Panzer, speechless. After a silent and awkward moment, Panzer finally spoke.

"Are you all right, Mr. Woodson?"

Quickly snapping out of it, Woodson shook his head and said, "Uh… yeah… I think so… could I please have a glass of water?"

"Certainly," said Panzer. He motioned to Ms. Jamison. "Carla, would you mind getting a glass of water for our guest?"

As Carla left the room, Panzer walked over to Woodson, stood beside him, and placed his hand on the archeologist's shoulder.

"Why me?" inquired Woodson glancing up at his host. "There are hundreds of archeologists who know Guatemala. I've only been there once… to Tikal. Anybody can tour Tikal; I did it on a Sunday afternoon. My expertise is the Yucatán Maya."

Panzer walked to the nearest glass case. "I understand they call you Woody?" Woodson nodded and Panzer continued, "Well Woody, tell me what you see here."

Woodson joined Panzer at the glass case. "My guess would be a glyph panel. One that was probably… let me get a closer look." Woodson put his nose right up to the glass. "A riser for a staircase, yes, I'm sure of it… probably one of many. I see figures of ballplayers … yes! This panel bears a remarkable resemblance to stelae found at Yaxchilán in Chiapas, Mexico. I'm sure of it!"

Panzer interrupted, "Can you date it, Woody?" he asked.

"Mid 700's A.D. would be my guess," replied Woodson with a smile of great satisfaction.

"You *are* as good as they say, Mr. Woodson!" declared Panzer. "I need *you* to lead this expedition."

Woodson stepped away from the glass and stared blankly into his host's confident eyes. There was no doubt in his mind that Panzer had something up his sleeve.

"I want you to look at one more stele, Woody," continued Panzer. "I'm sure you will find this one quite interesting."

Panzer led Woodson to a narrow steel door that was just to the left of the big oak desk. Panzer pulled out a full ring of keys. The free keys jingled loudly as the door quickly unlocked. The room was dark, smelled of something old, and damp. Panzer flipped a switch on the wall; suddenly the room illuminated, revealing a large stone stele. There was no glass case this time. It was too tall, at least two feet taller than Woodson.

"Can you read it, Woody?"

"May I touch it?"

Panzer nodded and made a polite gesture toward the stone. Woodson stepped carefully toward the weathered gray limestone. Reaching out, he ran his hands gently across the cold glyphs carved into the craggy surface. He had never seen one like this before. Nowhere in his travels or in his studies had he heard of any stele like this! His excitement was so great; he could barely catch his breath when he touched it.

"Can you read it?" Panzer asked again. This time however, his tone had grown impatient.

"I believe so, Mr. Panzer," replied Woodson never taking his eyes off the stele. "Can I get some tracing paper and a pencil? Oh, and a scratch pad too." Panzer motioned to Ms. Jamison and within moments, Woodson had everything that he had asked for.

The wars had greatly challenged my people. Food was scarce. The children went hungry. The walls of the city crumbled as the women cried for their husbands. Our army had been defeated time after time in the field of battle, the best men taken to the enemy's city. I feared their fate, for I believe they must have been sacrificed.

We did not ask for this war. The Toltec had come from the west to defeat us and take our cities. They sought the Sacred Cenote. They believed this deep well and the dark waters possessed some type of magic. Our culture seemed to have been of no concern to these animals. We had stripped the land of its goodness. The maize no longer grew. Water had become scarce. What have we done? The Toltecs seek only the Cenote. I, as ruler of this once great city, should have seen. I should have listened to the gods! We thought that we were invincible; that no man could defeat us. Was it I alone who believed this?

I had ordered the sacrifice of many children—sacrificed to the gods—thrown into the very cenote that our enemy covets. Somehow, I needed to satisfy the gods. Somehow, I had to save my people. I could not stand to watch the life bled from them another day. I had gone to the temple and walked the steps to pray. Maybe the gods could show my people the way back, to the better life that they have known.

That night I had a vision. Yum Caax, 'The Lord of the Forest,' called to me. The great god of plenty and riches that brings us maize, his gift of life, told me to lead my people away from our home. I must take them to the south, to a river—to a place where no man can harm my people again.

An hour passed before Woodson left the stele and stepped back into the office.

"Where did you get this?" he asked Panzer. Woodson's voice was firm.

"That's not important," Panzer replied stiffly. "What does it say? *What does it mean?*"

Without another word, Woodson handed his scribbled notes to Panzer. The collector snatched the notes and shuffled to his desk. There Panzer sat and devoured every word of translation that Woodson had scribbled.

"This is incredible," he cried. "Woody, do you have any idea what this means?"

"The ruler of Chichén Itzá, after losing the war with the Toltec, moved his people to a place of safety."

"Exactly!" cried Panzer. "On this stele begins the story of the lost city! Don't you see?"

"Yes, I do. But before we get too excited, I need to know where that stone came from."

Panzer could hardly contain his excitement. He paced around his desk finally dropping into his chair...

"Chichén Itzá!" he exclaimed. "The Sacred Cenote, that's where it all began!"

"No way Panzer," Woodson protested. "It's impossible that it came from Chichén Itzá..."

Panzer continued studying the paper. He completely ignored Woodson's protest.

"That stele is from Site Q, isn't it?"

"I'm almost sure of it!" exclaimed Panzer. He jumped from his chair. "Woodson, you must come with us. You have to lead this expedition!"

"I need to tell you about something else that happened last month." Woodson's hands trembled, small beads of sweat formed on his forehead and upper lip. "During our pursuit of the codex, something strange began happening to me. I began—"

"To have *visions*?" inquired Panzer, with an air of confidence.

"Yes... but how did you know?" he asked in disbelief.

"There is very little that I don't know about you. I know that you have experienced visions since you were a very young man. I also know that these visions were the same as Guerrero's himself."

Woodson's face paled and he stumbled backward. "How?" he asked incredulously.

"I also know that because of these visions, you somehow established a connection with Guerrero that transcended time itself."

Woodson's head was spinning—he needed to sit down. He cradled his head with his palms.

"A connection..." Panzer pressed on "... that helped lead you to The Fifth Codex." Panzer was well aware of how disturbed Woodson had become. "Forgive me, Woody, I didn't mean to upset you."

Carla handed the glass of water to Woodson. Glancing up, he smiled and took the glass. Then Woodson turned to Panzer. His gaze was cold, showing no emotion. "How could you know all those things about me?" he asked.

Then from the doorway came the sound of a familiar voice. "I told him, Woody!"

The glass dropped from Woodson's hand, spilling water all over the carpet. He turned toward the door.

"*Pedro*?" he gasped.

CHAPTER THREE
The Stele

It had been only two hours since sunrise. The jungle air felt like a wet blanket. As always, the jungle was hot, wet, and quiet. Only the cheerful caws of toucans and parrots broke the eerie silence that existed there. Soon, a new sound would fill the air: the harsh reverberation of a gas powered saw blade as it sliced through a thick, ancient slab of limestone.

The man ran the blade skillfully down the length of the weathered slab. The saw was loud and immediately caused the birds' playful calls to cease as they flew away to escape what had become an all too familiar noise. As the hours passed, the heat of the sun pounded against his already burning shoulders. Under the weight of the saw, he began to fatigue. Endless streams of sweat ran down his old but muscular arms while struggling to hold the saw steady. The only thing that kept him going was the promise of money. From this one dirty slab of limestone, he would earn enough to feed and clothe his family for many months, possibly the entire year. As the blade of his saw neared the end of its journey, he called out to another much younger man who was digging near by. The young man dropped his shovel and approached the limestone slab.

"Juan!" The man handling the saw had to yell over the grinding whine of the blade. "Bring the burlap bags."

Juan knew exactly what to do. Picking up the burlap sheets, he placed them gently at the foot of the limestone slab. The dust, as it flew from the saw cutting through the soft limestone, caused Juan to choke, but he never stopped working.

The cutter again yelled out to the young man. "Place your hands on each side… good… now bring your hands up a little bit higher. That is it! *Do not move!*"

Then as the whine of the saw finally ceased, the older man slowly came around the slab and knelt at the base, just in front of Juan.

"Bueno, my son," he said with a broad toothless smile. "It is free! Now move to that side and hold it. I will take this side." The two men moved into position. "On three, gently place the stele on the burlap with the glyphs facing up. Ready? One—two—*three*."

Slowly the two men flipped the limestone from its resting place and placed it on the soft burlap bedding that Juan had carefully arranged.

"Señor Smith will pay plenty for this one!" exclaimed the older man.

"Aren't you afraid that we will get caught?" asked Juan, feeling somewhat uncomfortable and strangely chilled on this hot day.

"How? Only the chicleros know about this place. We will make sure that the gringos do not find it."

"Can all the chicleros be trusted?" inquired the curious Juan. "Most are very poor since the gringos no longer need chicle to make their chewing gum."

"Do not worry," said the old man, reassuring Juan. "The other chicleros fear this place."

"I know, it scares me too," Juan replied, quickly glancing around the site. "Why are you not scared?"

"The fear of our family going without food is much greater than old legends."

Juan bent over the slab and ran his hand over the glyphs carved into the soft stone many centuries before. Though smoothed by the elements, the glyphs still told a story. The Mayan kings, or high priests, would have tales of their great victories in battle or wonderful accomplishments etched into these large limestone slabs. These stories were a legacy of the king's greatness. A legacy left for future generations.

"What do these drawings mean?" Juan asked.

"I am not certain," replied the older man, "But I believe I can read some of the symbols."

"You know of the old ways?" said the disbelieving Juan. "You can read these things that we sell?"

"It has been a long, long time since I studied the words of the ancients, but I will try."

The older man caressed the cold stone—glyph-by-glyph. As his hands moved gently across the stele, he would occasionally stop and speak the old words.

"The ruler of this city," he began, "these writings are his words."

"What does he say?" asked Juan, with the excited interest of a schoolchild.

"He says that his people came from the north. It was a very long journey. His ancestor, who also ruled these people, led them here. I think it says that if they had not come here, his people would have surely faced destruction."

He stopped reading and stepped back. Juan could plainly see the tears forming in the old man's eyes.

"What do you see?" inquired Juan. "Why do you cry?"

Slowly, the older man returned to the cold, dark stone and once again placed his hands upon the rough, gray surface.

"These people traveled a great distance to avoid destruction by a ruthless, horrible enemy. They built this great city and lived here for centuries while experiencing many hardships. They were here alone in this hidden place. They never had contact with any other cities again."

"Why does that sadden you?"

"It saddens me because we are here destroying their city. We destroy their legacy."

Suddenly there came a deep, raspy voice from behind.

"Not bad; for a *chiclero*."

The men jumped to their feet "Smith!" exclaimed the older chiclero upon seeing the intruder. Smith was of medium height with strong high cheekbones, deep sunken eyes and a neatly trimmed beard cut close to the jawbone.

"How did you find this place? I—"

"Never mind," replied Smith. "Just wrap that stele up... nice and neat."

"What about our money, Señor Smith? You have always paid me when I have delivered."

Smith placed his hands on his hips and began to laugh.

"You'll get your money when I'm good and ready to pay you!" he snapped.

Juan started toward Smith, but the older man grabbed his arm and said, "We will go to the authorities, Señor. We will not be cheated."

"And be arrested yourselves? I don't think so." Smith laughed again. Then he pulled a gun from under his vest and aimed it directly at Juan's head. "I would appreciate it if you gentlemen would pack that stone onto my burro. Hurry up. We can't keep the collectors waiting, *can we?*"

Woodson was in shock. Carla knelt down in front of his chair to pick up the empty glass.

"Are you all right, Mr. Woodson?" she inquired nervously.

Ignoring her question, Woodson stood and walked toward Pedro.

"What on earth are you doing here?" he asked.

Pedro looked into Woodson's eyes.

"Señor Panzer wanted *me* to lead this expedition," he began, "He didn't realize that I was only sixteen years old." Pedro ran his hand through his thick black hair and smiled. His toothy grin shined against his dark Mayan skin. "I told him that you were the only one to do it. I told him that if he wanted to succeed he needed you!"

"Why did you have to tell them about my visions?" Woodson said through clenched teeth. "How could that have mattered? Pedro, you are really pushing our friendship to the limit."

Panzer interrupted, "I need to know *everything* about the man who leads this expedition. I cannot take any chances. You have to understand that."

Woodson scratched his head before turning to Panzer.

"Why do you need to find this 'lost city,' Panzer?"

"The stelae, Woody!" exclaimed Panzer. "The chicleros in Guatemala are looting some of the most magnificent glyph-covered monuments anybody has ever seen. You have just seen one of the best samples ever found in a Mayan city. They are not coming from any known site, and they are certainly not coming from Mexico."

"How are they being smuggled out of Guatemala?" asked Woodson.

"A man named Smith. Dennis Smith. He knows how to get the artifacts from the looters."

"How?"

"We're not sure," replied Panzer thoughtfully. "But we *do* know what happens once he has them. Smith pays about a hundred dollars American for each stele, then they are loaded onto trucks and shipped over the border to Belize. There he meets with an agent who pays him four, maybe five times that amount. Next they are smuggled into Belgium and then back into the U.S.—"

Woodson quickly cut Panzer off. "Where they are sold to collectors like yourself for ten times that amount."

Panzer nodded and said, "Correct! So you see we need to stop the looting and destruction of all these Mayan treasures."

"You mean, like the ones here." Woody laughed as he waved his arm at the surrounding stelae to indicate that he had a good idea of how Panzer amassed his large collection.

"You're right, Woody," admitted Panzer sadly. "I'm as guilty as all of the other collectors. I've changed my mind on this whole thing. I think it's important that we find Site Q. and stop the destruction!"

"He's right, Woody," said Pedro. "We must find this city. If it truly exists, it could be the biggest archeological find ever!"

"Oh, it exists all right. I'm sure of it," added Panzer. "It's probably in the Petén region of Guatemala. The far northern region has many sites. There are at least twenty-six known sites. Of these sites, they have studied only fourteen. My guess is that there might be another thirty sites yet undiscovered."

"And you think that the site where this stele was found is one of them?"

"Yes, I do." Panzer walked over to a map that hung against the wall. The map showed the northern region of Guatemala. Panzer pointed toward the Mexican border. "It's somewhere here in this area. I'm sure of it."

Woodson walked over to the map.

"That's near La Corona," he said. "Hasn't it already been determined that La Corona was *not* Site Q?"

Panzer reached into his pocket and pulled out a shard of pottery. As if it were a precious jewel, he carefully handed the reddish clay piece to Woodson.

"Have you seen anything like this before?"

Woodson held it up to the light. It could not have been more than four inches square.

"Pottery, codex shard," he replied. "Sure I've seen plenty…Wait!" Woodson pulled it closer for further examination. "I've never seen one like this. Is this a map? Panzer, where did you get this?"

"Looks like you're not the only one who gets messages from the past, eh Woodson?" Panzer remarked with a smirk.

Woodson glared at Panzer.

"Sorry," said Panzer sheepishly.

"If I decide to take the job, which I haven't, who will be going on this expedition?"

"You, me, Pedro and Ms. Jamison," replied Panzer.

"Pedro?" snapped Woodson. "He's just a kid!"

"He wants to go," replied Panzer. "I see no problem—"

"No problem," cried Woodson in disbelief. "This could be dangerous!"

"C'mon Woody," said Pedro. "It can't be any more dangerous than what happened at Chichén Itzá!"

Woodson shook his head and sighed. "I should know better than this. If I agree to do this, I want Professor Lyons and Blue to come with us as well."

"Agreed!" cried Panzer with delight. "No problem, Woody. I want anybody that can help us find that city."

"We'll also need a shaman; a holy man that knows the old *and* new ways of the Maya."

Panzer shot Woodson a puzzled look.

"The Maya depend on shamans for everything: weddings, funerals, contacting spirits, and sacrifices. If it's all right with you, I'll arrange for one to meet us down there."

"Agreed!"

"Since you've agreed to all of my terms," began Woodson, "then all that's left is for me to sleep on it. I *will* make up my mind by tomorrow. I will call you in the morning. Pedro," Woodson snapped at his young apprentice. "Grab your hat. You are coming home with me! You and I have *a lot* to discuss!"

CHAPTER FOUR
The Expedition Begins

"You're going *where*?" demanded Blue.

"Guatemala. And you're going, too," replied Woodson, smiling.

"What about Lyons? He wanted you to stay home and rest."

"Umm... he's going too."

"When did you decide to go?"

"Just this morning," Woodson replied, trying not to grin too broadly.

Blue turned toward Pedro and roared, "I just know that you're at the bottom of this, Pedro Garcia. You know that Woody needs his rest. How could you do this without...?" Blue turned back to Woodson. "And you... you *could* say no!"

Woodson wrapped his arm around Blue and led her over to the couch. He and Pedro explained what they might be up against in Guatemala, and the archeological importance of finding Site Q.

"Okay, okay. Who else is going on this expedition, anyway?" she snapped.

"Well, there's Pedro," began Woodson, "Angel, if he can get away, Lyons, Mr. Panzer, and Ms. Jamison. And you, of course."

"I don't think so, Woody," barked Blue impatiently. "You nearly got me killed in Chichén Itzá. If you insist on going, you can go without me! Understand?"

"Blue, I need you on this one," Woodson pleaded. "If we find this lost city, there will be *way* more to do than Pedro, Lyons and I can handle. You *are* a skilled archeologist—one of the best. Without you, we may never have known how to stop Aguilar. I—"

The ringing of the doorbell interrupted Woodson. Without a word, he gave Blue a shrug and headed for the front door. As he made his way across the house, Woodson could hear Blue directing her tirade at poor Pedro. He opened the door to find the attractive Ms. Jamison, whom he had met the day before.

"Ms. Jamison. What can I do for you?" he asked, surprised to see her.

"Please, call me Carla," she answered with an alluring smile.

"Certainly, Carla, what brings you here?" Woodson gestured for her to enter. "Please come in."

"Mr. Panzer wanted me to bring you this envelope. It contains all of your travel arrangements," she replied.

"Thanks. Hey, why don't you come in and meet Blue?"

"I think I might be interrupting something," said Carla. She peeked timidly around the corner. Blue was still giving young Pedro a good going over and was making no effort to keep her voice down. "Look, I'll just be—"

"Don't be silly," said Woodson. "That's just Blue. Her bark is a lot worse than her bite, c'mon in."

Woodson enthusiastically grabbed Carla by the arm and led her into the living room. Blue was still protesting to Pedro that she had no intention of going on this 'silly' expedition.

"Blue," said Woodson, attempting to interrupt. Blue was in rare form today. No one was going to get a word in until she was ready.

"If you and Woody have *any* sense at all..."

"Oh, Blue!" Woodson said a little louder.

"... You will tell this—Panzer character—that you have no intention of..."

"BLUE," shouted Woodson.

"*What?*" Blue turned to see Woodson standing there arm in arm with the very attractive Ms. Jamison.

"Blue, I want you to meet Carla Jamison. Carla, this is Blue."

Blue walked directly over to Woodson, grabbed his arm, and led him into the next room. "Please excuse us, Ms. Jamison," said Blue, as politely as she could, all the while glaring at Carla over her shoulder.

"Is that *the Ms. Jamison? As in, the Ms. Jamison that is going with you to Guatemala?*" asked Blue, once they were safely in the next room. Woodson could not help but notice the look of jealousy spreading quickly across Blue's face.

"Yep!" replied Woodson trying not to smile.

"Kind of pretty isn't she? You know, in an athletic kind of way," commented Blue.

"Yep, she sure is."

"You know, Woody," said Blue nonchalantly. "I don't think it's a good idea for you to go on this expedition alone."

"I won't be alone, Blue," Woodson said playfully. "Pedro and Lyons will be there, Mr. Panzer... and of course, Carla will be there too."

"Look, Woody, I think I'd better go with you," said Blue, as if she had not heard a word. "You had a pretty rough go of it in Mexico. Yes... I think it would definitely be better if I tagged along."

"But, you were quite emphatic about not going on this 'silly' expedition." Woodson was beyond trying to hold back the big smile spreading across his face. Blue did not notice.

"Well, I've changed my mind." Blue took Woodson by the hand and squeezed it tightly. "Now let's go meet your, *Ms Jamison*, shall we? We don't want to be rude, do we?"

CHAPTER FIVE
Belize

A dark figure sat quietly at a table in a shadowy corner of the run down cantina. Dennis Smith never really enjoyed his trips to Belize. One never knew whom you might run into, especially if your occupation was smuggling illegal artifacts. Smith knew this cantina well—it was one of the few places he felt safe from the police. This hole in the wall was off the beaten path and usually frequented by two kinds of people: those interested in selling and those looking to buy.

As a pretty señorita placed another whisky on Smith's table, two rough looking men entered. This was not Smith's first experience with this pair; he knew them much better than he cared to. Right now, they were his only link to getting the stolen goods off the continent. Smith motioned to the barmaid for two more whiskies and stood to greet his guests. He called them Hans and Franz. He did not know their real names. He did not want to; it would be too dangerous. They were old sailors, merchants that would deal in anything for a profit.

"Gentlemen, please join me," Smith said, extending his hand in friendship.

Hans was the larger of the two men. He had broad shoulders, a barrel chest, topped by a puffy, bearded face. The smaller of the two, Franz, slightly built wearing a full beard, was obviously the smarter one. He was dressed quite neatly and carried himself with an air of confidence.

"Well Smith… That *is* your name this week. Isn't it?" asked Franz, looking Smith up and down.

"Franz. So good to see you again, I—"

"Never mind that, show me what you've got," Franz barked impatiently.

"Sit down, Gentlemen," Smith replied cautiously. He quickly realized that the smaller man was in no mood for false niceties. Smith liked the fact that Franz got right down to business. "I'll show you the best piece I've found so far." He reached under his chair and pulled out a small pouch. Slowly removing a small photograph, he handed it to Franz.

Franz stroked his beard while he viewed the photo.

"Very interesting," he said, handing the photo to his large friend. "You are quite right. This might just be the best yet." Franz continued to stroke his beard. He eyed Smith suspiciously. "How much?" he inquired.

"Two thousand—American," Smith replied coldly.

"Too much!" interrupted Hans.

Franz held up his hand to silence his companion. "That is more than twice as much as your usual price. Why?"

"This is the best one yet! Take it or leave it!" Smith exclaimed. He reached across the table and snatched the photo from Hans' grip.

"What do *you* think we can get for this, Smith?" asked Hans.

"Plenty!" he replied. "At least five to six thousand dollars, this thing could bring as much as fifty thousand in the states, maybe more in auction."

Hans and Franz leaned toward each other. They spoke softly in an attempt to keep Smith from hearing, but Smith's hearing was quite acute.

"I think you gentlemen need to learn to speak a little softer. What is it with you sailors? You're so loud!" Smith shook his head and smiled. "Now, if you would be so kind as to remove all weapons from your person, and gently... very gently, place them on the table."

"What are you talking about?" Franz inquired. "We were just discussing the price. You know—"

"Save it, Franz," Smith snapped. "I've known you guys a long time. Remember. I was the one who helped you smuggle the weapons in during the civil war. Just do as I said." Smith was losing his patience. "Now!" he exclaimed through gritted teeth.

"Why should we?" asked Hans.

"I have two friends under this table aimed at your friend, Franz," Smith replied coldly. "You might have heard of them, Smith and Wesson. Do we understand? *Slowly!*"

The sailors reached under their jackets and pulled out their handguns. Reluctantly, they placed the black, snub-nosed weapons onto the table.

"Thank you, gentlemen," Smith said softly. He pulled the weapons to his side of the table. "Shall we say... two thousand, American? Meet me tonight at our usual place of business, in the usual manner."

Franz, his eyes narrowed with anger, reluctantly agreed with a brusque nod.

"Excellent. Ten o'clock then?"

Franz nodded again. "What about our guns?" he asked, glancing across the table at the weapons.

"Just leave them right where they are until I'm out that door," replied Smith pointing toward the entrance.

Franz nodded again.

"Where are we going, Woody?" Blue asked as she stepped out of the cab nearly tripping over the high curb.

"I think the hotel is just around the corner," replied Woodson, while helping Pedro remove the bags from the trunk of the car. "Yeah, there it is. C'mon!"

"What time is it here, anyway? Is Belize on the same time as Chicago?" she asked. "Boy, this street is dark."

"I think it's about ten o'clock, Blue," said Pedro. He held up his watch hoping to find light somewhere on this dark street.

Woody stopped at the door to the hotel. It was an old building, typical of the lodging available in Belize City. Belize is unique in Central America. Originally conquered by the Spanish, then years later settled by English woodcutters. As the English population grew, Spain found itself unable to maintain control over the territory. The war with England in the 1700's had put further strain on Spain's ability to govern the region. Eventually, Central America emancipated from Spanish rule. In 1836, the British claimed the area, creating a blend of cultures (English, Spanish and Maya), quite different from its Spanish speaking neighbors. Looking down the dark, deserted street, Woodson eyed a small cantina that appeared to be open.

"Why don't you guys go check us in," said Woodson, placing his bags in front of the hotel door. There's a little cantina down the street. I'll go and get us some food. Who's hungry?"

"*Food!* It's about time. I'm starving!" exclaimed Blue.

"What a surprise," said Pedro. He knew from experience that Blue was *always* hungry.

Woodson watched as Blue and Pedro entered the hotel before starting for the cantina. The area was quiet. The air was wet and warm; the clean, fresh, familiar smell of the sea filled Woodson's senses. He heard the bells signaling the time from the ships in the harbor. Woodson never tired of the Caribbean. The sights, the sounds, and the people always made him realize how good life could be.

The cantina was nearly empty. The only customers were two bearded sailors huddled together at a table in the corner of the room. The place was dark and smelled of beer and smoke, but as luck would have it, served food as well as drinks.

The dark skinned server, who stood behind a high, bar-like counter greeted Woodson with a warm smile. While placing his order, Woodson noticed the two men in the corner getting up to leave. Woodson smiled and greeted them with a tip of his hat, but they walked right by as if they had not noticed. He shrugged it off and started making small talk with the server.

Heading back toward the hotel Woodson noticed that the same two men he had seen in the cantina appeared to be arguing with a third man. As Woodson drew closer, the three men realized that he had witnessed their altercation. The two men dressed as sailors quickly disappeared into the shadows while the third man jumped into a nearby van. The van pulled quickly away from the curb, tires squealing against the damp surface—headed directly for Woodson. With only a split second to act, he jumped out of the vans way as it sped by.

Woodson lay there, sprawled out over the cobblestone street, barely able to catch his breath. The van suddenly came to a screeching halt. Now in reverse, the car sped back toward him. This time the driver, careful not to hit him, pulled next to the still helpless Woodson. The bearded driver peered down at the damp street. The steely stare sent a shiver up Woodson's spine. The driver's eyes narrowed, as if he were trying to recognize Woodson. He could not. Woodson glared back—reading the man's features. Before Woodson could get to his feet, the bearded man smiled, revved the engine until its whiney roar echoed through the nearly deserted streets, and sped off into the night.

CHAPTER SIX
Guatemala

"How much longer, Woody?" asked Blue, who was busy peering out the window of the small twin-engine craft flying them to Guatemala.

Woodson was sitting on the other side of the plane taking in the sights.

"We should be landing in Santa Elena in about ten minutes," he replied absently.

"Great! What's it like there?" she asked.

"Angel brought me here when I was nine years old," Pedro replied, his nose glued to the window. "I don't remember much except that it looked like a very old city with roads that have never been paved. I remember lots of dust—everywhere."

Blue glanced out her window before turning to Pedro. "Anything to do there?" she asked.

"I think there are lots of restaurants," replied Pedro, still unable to pull his face from the plane's tiny window.

"Well, it can't be all that bad, can it?" joked Blue. "Seriously, what happens when we get there?"

"We meet Lyons tomorrow. Panzer and Carla the day after—" Woodson was quickly interrupted.

"You mean *Ms. Jamison?*" she corrected coldly.

Woodson pretended to shiver. Blue was still feeling some pangs of jealousy and Woodson was actually enjoying it.

"Tomorrow, we take a walk to the Caves of Actun-Can, not very far from town," he said.

"Why?" she asked.

"To meet, Keh, the shaman Angel recommended."

"Why do we need this guy?"

"We're in an environment that we know *nothing* about. Keh can help by knowing the local customs. He's lived in this region his entire life."

"But—"

"And...Angel said that Keh understands the old ways."

"I understand, Woody. I—"

"Last, Angel felt that Keh might be able to sort out my problem."

Blue turned toward Woodson and looked deep into his eyes.

"You have no problem," protested Blue. "All of that stuff's over with. It ended at Chichén Itzá!"

Woodson looked away and fell silent. He was not so sure.

"What are the Caves of Actun-Can?" inquired Pedro, attempting to change the subject. Woodson snapped out of it and gave him a smile.

"The English translation is The Cave of the Serpent," began Woodson. "It's basically a limestone cave formation where tourists go to in hopes of seeing a *real serpent*. Keh is the cave keeper and he wants us to meet him there. Then we pack up and take a bus to the eastern highlands and El Naranjo."

"*Bus?*" Blue inquired with interest. "What do you *mean* a bus? You never said a word about a bus ride. I—"

Woodson quickly interrupted. "Relax Blue, it's going to be just fine."

"Oh, no you don't, Richard Woodson," she snapped. "I've heard about the chicken buses down here. Rusty old school buses... overloaded with passengers... and chickens, lots and lots of chickens."

Woodson and Pedro started to laugh.

"Panzer assured me that we would be on a Pullman bus with air conditioning and bathrooms," said Woodson. "You'll be fine! Relax."

Blue did not say another word until after they landed in Santa Elena.

Early the next morning Woodson found himself in the lobby of the Hotel Sac-Nicté, in search of a cup of coffee. The hotel was modern and there was a restaurant on the premises, which was a rarity in this part of the world. The smell of fresh coffee and tortillas led him straight to it. As Woodson sat at a table enjoying his first cup of the day, his thoughts began to wander.

This being his first time in this part of Guatemala, he thought about how different the landscape here was to the thorny brush jungle of the Yucatan Peninsula. It rained quite a lot in this region and the jungles appeared dense and lush green from the constant humidity.

Santa Elena, a small community on the banks of Lago de Petén Itzá, was the best point of departure for any expedition to the Rio Usamacinta. Buses ran regularly to El Naranjo, near the Sierra del Lacondón National Park. This was the area where Panzer felt certain the lost city would be located.

It was only seven-thirty in the morning and very few people were moving about in the hotel or the restaurant. Blue and Pedro were still asleep. The trip had already been difficult and the heat, at times, nearly intolerable. Woodson had not been able to sleep. In all his years of studies and practical experience, his dream of discovering an ancient archeological site had always been his greatest.

Woodson was completely lost in thought, quite unaware that his old friend and mentor, Professor Lyons, had entered the restaurant. Lyons, Woodson's long time associate, was a rugged-looking man in his mid sixties. The professor's once thick, blond hair had faded white and his tanned, wrinkled skin matched the appearance of any man who had spent as many years in the intense Central American sun as he had. Lyons was extremely spry for his age. Being thin and wiry obviously kept the professor young and vibrant. Even Woodson, who was just over half the professor's age, had trouble keeping up with 'the old man' on those long, hot days restoring the Mayan ruins at Chichén Itzá

"Woody!" Lyons cried out. His voice sounded tired and raspy. "How are you?"

Woodson looked up from his steaming, black coffee and smiled. It was good to see his old friend again, especially under better circumstances. The adventure in the Yucatan had put them on opposing sides. Lyons had found Gonzalo Guerrero's journal at Tulum, but was having great difficulty translating it due to its mysterious mixture of Mayan and old world Spanish. Guerrero, the first Spaniard to live among the Maya, had kept a journal of his life in the Yucatan. It was thought that this journal could lead to a mysterious codex, or book, that could connect the two worlds of the Maya—the living and the dead.

Three years prior to Lyons' discovering Guerrero's journal, he had found another—a journal left at Chichén Itzá by Guerrero's enemy, Geronimo Aguilar. The modern Aguilar, his descendant, had somehow heard about Lyons' spectacular find. Aguilar contacted the professor and promised to pay a substantial amount of money if he could translate the journal. Aguilar was sure that Geronimo Aguilar's journal would lead him to The Fifth Codex, the sacred Maya book that would give him eternal life.

Geronimo Aguilar's journals failed to tell of where Guerrero hid The Fifth Codex. It was not until three years later, when they found Guerrero's journal, did it prove the existence of the mysterious codex.

Lured by the promise of money, the kind of money that a professor of archeology could never possibly make, Lyons, knowing his former student's incredible curiosity, devised a clever plan to trick Woodson into translating Guerrero's journals and ultimately tracking down The Fifth Codex.

Professor Lyons convinced young Pedro to pretend that *he* had found Gonzalo Guerrero's journal at the ruined city of Tulum. Pedro, thinking that he was acting in Woodson's best interest, convinced his friend that he had found the journal. Woodson, whose expertise was Mayan hieroglyphics and old world Spanish, could not possibly resist the opportunity to translate Guerrero's journals.

Realizing that Aguilar was completely mad, Lyons soon came to his senses just in time for he and his friends to stop Aguilar from releasing the unknown evils that dwelt deep within the codex.

"Lyons!" Woodson exclaimed. He held up his steaming cup. "Can I get you some of this?" he asked.

"You bet!" Lyons replied enthusiastically, before turning to the waiter. "A shot of Kahlua liqueur, señor?" he inquired. The waiter smiled and nodded. "Gracias, mi amigo," said Lyons.

"It's seven-thirty in the morning," said Woodson, hardly able to believe that his old friend was about to have alcohol at such an early hour. "Are you crazy?"

"It's gotta be five p.m. somewhere," he replied. "Man, I traveled all night to get here. Give a guy a break!" Lyons gave Woodson a warm handshake before sitting. "How are you, Woody?" he asked. Lyons was still very concerned about Woodson's state of mind. "Have you gotten over our last little adventure?"

"Actually I'm feeling pretty good," replied Woodson before taking a sip from his cup.

"That was a rough time," began Lyons, "another couple of inches and you and Blue would have been goners."

"I'm sure that you and Pedro would have saved us even if we had fallen into the well."

"That cenote at Chichén Itzá is pretty deep and dark. I'm not so sure—"

Woodson quickly interrupted his old friend. "I am," he said. Lyons smiled.

"What's the deal on this guy Panzer?" asked Lyons, thankfully watching his cup of coffee being place on the table. "I've heard that he's one of the biggest collectors around. Is he on the level?"

"You know about Site Q, right?"

Lyons nodded. "Who doesn't?"

"Good." Woodson's tone turned serious. "Then you know about the mysterious artifacts being auctioned off in New York. Panzer says he knows where they're coming from."

"Only the chicleros know that," responded Lyons, "The chicleros and the bad guys who buy the artifacts. How does *he* know where this site is?"

"He has a map on a codex pottery shard. He's sure that this is the real thing."

"Did you see it?"

"Yeah, but he didn't let me get a real good look. He just made some crack about me not being the only one who receives messages from the past."

"Isn't he the comedian." Lyons took a sip of his Mexican coffee and smiled. "Now I can face the day. What's next?"

"We're going to the Caves of Actun-Can to meet our shaman."

Lyons pretended to look frightened. "Sounds mysterious and dangerous," he replied sarcastically.

"Keh, our shaman, is the caretaker at the caves. Actun-Can means, Cave of the Serpent... or something like that."

"Ooh, I'm impressed."

"Sorry, Professor," said Woodson shaking his head at his friend's attempt at humor. "Nobody has ever seen a serpent there; it's just another tourist trap. There are limestone formations in the shapes of animals and humans. The legend is that if you look at them long enough, they will depict scenes from the distant past. I guess if you look at anything long enough it will look like something else. Anyway, I understand the entrance is a good spot for a picnic."

"A picnic?" asked Lyons sarcastically. "If there's food, Blue should love it there."

"Angel said this guy Keh is the real deal."

"That's good enough for me. What do you say we go wake up Blue and Pedro. I'll even treat them to some breakfast."

"What time do the caves open?" asked Blue. They were nearly to the entrance to Actun-Can. "My feet are killing me! I thought it was a short walk from town."

"Quit complaining!" snapped Woodson, shaking his head. "Angel said that it opens at eight a.m. Keh told him that it is rare for anyone to show before ten. We should have plenty of time to meet Keh and make all of the arrangements."

As the group arrived at the entrance, a small, dark man with a sparse, bristly mustache and beard greeted them. The old man was dressed in a brightly colored shirt, red scarf, and a floppy straw hat. His eyes were small, very dark, and he had a crooked nose. It appeared as if it had been broken more than once.

"Buenos dias mi amigo's... ahhh... amiga." The old man smiled at Blue revealing a missing front tooth.

Woodson stepped forward and held out his hand.

"I'm Richard Woodson. We are supposed to meet Keh, the cave keeper. Is he here, Señor?"

The old man took Woodson's hand in his. He gazed deeply into the younger man's eyes. The two men stood in silence, the air around them felt still and uncomfortable. Even the others could feel it. Something was happening, but no one was sure what it was. Suddenly, a swirling wind swept through the tall trees that shaded the tiny entrance to the caves from the bright morning sun. There was a sweet smell—a fresh, almost cleansing breeze, unlike anything Woodson had experienced before.

Finally, the wind died down. The small man smiled while continuing to squeeze Woodson's outstretched hand.

"Angel was right, Professor Woodson. The spirits *are* still with you!"

Woodson drew his hand from the man's. Cautiously, he backed away. Woodson felt faint and disorientated. The others stood in silence not knowing what to do.

"*You* must be Keh," said Woodson, regaining his composure.

"Yes. You have found the one you seek, Señor, as have I!"

CHAPTER SEVEN
Suspicion

Okay, Woody, can you tell me what all of that was about?" asked Blue, as they started down the narrow jungle-lined path that would take them back to town. "This Keh guy gives me the creeps!"

"I'm not sure I know what that old shaman was talking about," replied Woodson, while pulling Blue out of the way as an Iguana scurried out of the brush and onto the road. "Angel told me that we need this guy and that's good enough for me!"

Lyons grabbed Woodson by the arm and spun him around.

"That guy knows more about you then you're letting on," snapped the professor. "We all felt something back there when you two shook hands and you know it. I thought you were going to pass out!"

Woodson hesitated. The morning clouds were breaking up and the heat from the fully exposed sun felt good as it bathed his face. Woodson was well aware that something strange had indeed happened back at the cave. The feelings from his quest for The Fifth Codex had returned with just a simple touch of the old man's hand. Maybe Keh and Angel were right. Maybe the spirits did still dwell deep within. This Keh character scared Woodson, but he could not let on to the others. Angel was always right. Woodson needed to trust Keh—possibly with all of their lives!

"I'm fine. I just felt a little faint for a second, that's all," he finally said.

"I saw the look in your eyes when he touched you, Woody. You *know* that I've seen that look before," added

Pedro, who stood face to face with his mentor. "Are you sure it's a good idea to have this man with us?"

Woodson placed both hands on his young friend's shoulders and replied, "Keh was *your* grandfather's idea. This is just an archeological expedition. What could happen?" Woodson was not certain whether he was trying to convince his friends or himself. "Now, could we please get back to town? We're due to meet Panzer and Carla—"

"*Ms. Jamison!*" Blue quickly narrowed one eye at Woodson.

"Ms. Jamison," Woodson swiftly added to satisfy the uncharacteristically jealous Blue, "In about one hour."

"I thought we were taking a Pullman?" growled Blue. She and Woodson squeezed down the aisle of the crowded bus. The bus was loaded with locals, sometimes with as many as four to a seat. There were women with crying babies cradled in their arms, men smoking long smelly cigars, and leashed goats sitting in the narrow aisle. The bus looked old and worn. It had undoubtedly seen many hard miles. The cloth seats were threadbare and there was graffiti all over the roof, walls and windows. Blue hoped that the irritating smells from the animals and the hanging smoke would dissipate once the bus pulled away.

Woodson looked back, smiled, and said, "This *is* the Pullman, Blue."

"Looks like a Chicken Bus to me," she groaned.

"Can't be," he said with a chuckle. "There isn't one chicken on this bus! Anyway, chicken busses are old school busses. This is... or used to be a luxury Pullman! There's Panzer and Ca—Ms. Jamison in those seats up ahead. Those must be our seats there." Woodson peeked around Blue looking for Pedro. "Did you get our gear stowed okay?"

"Si, Woody," replied Pedro, carefully squeezing by one of the many goats that occupied the bus' aisle.

Woodson and Blue took the seats directly in front of Panzer and Ms. Jamison. Pedro and Lyons tried to get comfortable in the seat directly across the aisle, but a woman and her screaming baby sat between Lyons and the window. The infant kept grabbing at Lyon's face.

"Ah, Mr. Woodson," said Panzer once everyone was seated. "So glad you could make it. This must be Blue."

Woodson made all the introductions as the bus pulled away to begin the five-hour journey to El Naranjo. Woodson shifted in his seat so he and Panzer could further discuss what lay ahead for their little group of explorers.

"Where is your shaman?" inquired Panzer.

"Keh will join us tomorrow afternoon," replied Woodson, trying to talk over the crying baby and snorting goats. "I don't want to yell over all the noise, Mr. Panzer, but I need to know more about that map on that pottery shard."

"There will be plenty of time for that. I would prefer not to discuss it now."

"What happens when we get to El Naranjo?" Woodson inquired, hoping that Panzer could hear.

Panzer leaned toward Woodson so he would not have to yell. "I have two vehicles waiting there to pick us up. From there, we will go to a campsite near the San Pedro River to await the arrival of your shaman."

"You already have people in place there?" asked Woodson. He was not aware that there were any others involved. He could not hide his surprise or dissatisfaction upon finding out.

"Of course, Woody," replied Panzer, ignoring Woodson's obvious dissatisfaction. "Hernándo is there taking care of things. From Cozumel originally... good man, knows the region well." Panzer smiled and turned his attention to Carla Jamison, who had been sitting there quietly taking in the colorful local flavor the bus provided.

Woodson looked across the aisle to check on Lyons and Pedro. The professor was holding a screaming baby, while Pedro was helping the mother locate her bag. Lyons looked terrified and held the child up and as far away as his arms would allow. Woodson smiled. He knew how babies scared the professor. When he turned toward Blue to point out the professor's dilemma, Woodson found her staring face to face with a baby goat.

"Woody!" she exclaimed, looking absolutely petrified. "Get this *thing* out of my face!" The goat moved within an inch of Blue's nose.

Woodson laughed and said, "Just switch seats with me. I'll handle it."

Blue carefully scooted up on Woodson's lap. She then slipped down onto his side of the seat as he scooted over. Now, face to face with Blue's new friend, Woodson took a deep breath and blew right up the goat's nose. It quickly turned away.

"How did you know that would work?" asked an amused Blue.

"Dunno," he replied with a shrug, "works great on dogs." Woodson pointed across the aisle at the-panic stricken, baby-holding Lyons. The infant was screaming and kicking its feet. The professor looked petrified. Pedro and the baby's mother were having no luck finding a fresh diaper in the mother's carpetbag. Even the goats were becoming restless. "Do you think we should go across the aisle there and give the professor and Pedro a hand? It looks like they could use a little help."

"You sit. I'll see if I can rescue the two big strong men from the itty, bitty baby," Blue said with a giggle.

Woodson shook his head and leaned toward the window. The sun had gone behind the clouds and the air had filled with a foggy mist. As the bus made its way through the steamy jungle, Woodson's mind began to wander. Shutting out the noise and clatter in the bus, his thoughts again turned to the exciting prospect of finding a lost city. Deeper and deeper in thought he fell until suddenly, he felt the bus lurch and swerve to the side of the road. Woodson snapped out of his reverie. He spotted a vehicle with a driver and two passengers pass the bus. As it did, the driver glanced up at the bus, making eye contact with Woodson. It was him—the man who had nearly run him over in Belize. It was obvious by the look on his face that the bearded man had recognized Woodson as well.

The car pulled dangerously close to the bus so the bearded man could make direct eye contact with Woodson. Then, with a wave and a smile, he pulled the vehicle safely away from the bus and sped off. Again, Woodson was certain that this was not the last time that he would see that face. They *would* meet again.

Upon arriving at the small village of El Naranjo, the group met their guide, Hernándo. He was much larger then the natives Woodson were accustomed to seeing in Mexico. Nearly six feet tall with a large upper body, Hernándo was an imposing figure. Panzer moved quickly to his side to discuss the arrangements for departure.

Meanwhile Pedro had climbed up on top of the bus to unload their baggage.

"Be careful with the instruments, Pedro!" said Lyons, waiting patiently for Pedro to hand down the cases.

"This one is Woody's, Professor! Here it comes!"

As Pedro carefully handed down a long aluminum case, it slipped from Lyons' hands and crashed to the ground. The impact caused the case to open, revealing a polished, black, recurve style bow and at least a dozen arrows.

"That looks medieval," observed Blue. She knelt down and ran her hand curiously along the weapon's polished, sloping curves. "Why'd you bring this, Woody?" she inquired, nervously voicing the question that must have been on everyone's mind.

Blue pulled her hand away from the bow as Woodson quickly bent over and shut the case.

"This is not the Yucatan, people," he said. Woodson smiled but his tone was quite serious. "You all knew there was risk involved in coming here."

"Do you really think that we're going to need weapons?" asked Blue, arms folded tightly across her chest. Blue shivered as if she had just felt a cold breeze.

"Just a precaution, I wasn't even going to tell you about it!" he replied.

"Bow and arrows eh?" inquired Panzer, glancing over Woodson's shoulder at the tightly shut case. "Can you use them?" he asked.

"Second place in all of *the* U.S." replied Woodson proudly, "college nationals. I think I can handle it okay!"

"Well, I'd feel a lot better had you finished first!" chided Panzer.

"Me too!" added Woodson. Everybody had a good laugh except Pedro, who was still on top of the bus. The young apprentice felt a chill run down his spine, not cold but familiar. Pedro shook it off and continued to unload the gear.

After a short drive through the jungle, they pulled up to a small campsite just outside a little village.

"Not much around these parts, Panzer!" exclaimed Woodson, stepping out of the car and looking about the small thatched huts that dotted the jungle around them. "Who lives in the huts?"

"No, not much around here, but this is the best place to start from," replied Panzer. He then looked toward the huts. "Must be chicleros living there." Panzer pointed toward the north. "Hernándo says that we need to follow the river for about ten miles or so. Then, as the river turns north into Mexico, we head southwest toward the National Park— Sierra del Lacandón."

"Then, what?" asked Woodson while surveying the Rio (river) San Pedro.

Hernándo, the large Mayan guide, suddenly appeared at Woodson's side.

"Then, Señor Woodson," he said, "we travel to the Usamacinta River and find your so-called *lost city*!" Hernándo's tone was cynical sprinkled with a hint of mean.

"So, Hernándo, you don't believe there is a lost city," said Panzer giving Woodson a wink.

Hernándo suddenly turned very serious.

"The Petén holds many secrets and many legends. The gods protect them from outsiders."

"You're an outsider. You're from Cozumel, are you not?" asked Blue.

The group began to gather around Hernándo.

"That is correct, Señorita," replied the large man. "But I am of the Maya. I share the blood of the Itzás; the greatest of all the Maya."

Is that why you live here instead of Mexico?" pressed Blue.

"The señorita asks too many questions, I think," replied Hernándo before going back to unloading the cars.

"Woody, that guy gives me the creeps too," said Blue with a shudder. "Are all of the people down here as strange as he and that Keh character we met earlier?"

47

"This place is different from Mexico," replied Woodson. "This country has recently ended a thirty-year civil war. The government killed thousands of Mayans during *The Rebellion,* literally tearing this country apart. It has only been a few years since the fighting stopped. The healing could take a long, long time."

"Excuse me," Carla Jamison interrupted, "could you please help me with my bags," she asked gently placing her hand on the archeologist's shoulder.

"Sure, Carla... I mean, Ms. Jamison," Woodson replied sheepishly trying not to make eye contact with Blue. "I would be happy to."

Blue rolled her eyes and asked, "Pedro, do you think she's pretty?"

"Who?" responded Pedro.

"Ms. Jamison, you big dope," she said shaking her head. "Who did you think I was talking about?"

Young Pedro simply shrugged his shoulders and smiled.

The night proved uneventful. Everyone was exhausted from the long bus ride and the unrelenting heat and humidity; it was not long after the sun had set behind the tall, thickly treed jungle that they all made for their tents and hopefully a goodnights rest.

Woodson pushed the tent flap away from the opening. The camp was still very quiet with only Hernándo up and about building a large fire to prepare breakfast.

"Good morning, Hernándo," Woodson called out, as he squeezed through the narrow opening. The large Mayan did not reply. "What's for breakfast?" This time Hernándo mustered up a barely audible grunt and threw another log onto the already blazing fire. "This should be interesting," Woodson said to himself softly

After a quiet breakfast, Hernándo did little more than grunt in reply to anything he was asked. Woodson accompanied Hernándo back to El Naranjo to meet Keh's bus. Again, Woodson tried to strike up a conversation with his companion, but after a series of grunts and single syllable answers, Woodson happily gave up.

When they arrived at the village, the bus from Santa Elena still had not. Woodson decided to leave the reticent Hernándo at the stop to wait for Keh's bus so he could take in the sites. There was certainly not much to see. El Naranjo was far from a bustling Guatemalan metropolis. Left over from the war, large deserted army barracks took up most of the village. El Naranjo was just a sleepy little town, especially this early in the morning. As Woodson walked by the barracks, he heard a shrill voice call his name.

"Señor, Woodson! Señor, Woodson!" A high-pitched, thickly accented voice called out from down the road.

Woodson turned to see a small dark man dressed in white running toward him waving a small piece of paper over his head.

"Si... I am Woodson."

By the time the small man reached Woodson, he was completely out of breath and could hardly speak.

"Is... Señor... Panzer... here... with... you?" he inquired. With every word, the little man struggled to catch his breath.

"No. Who are you?"

"Pardon me," he replied, before taking a long, deep breath. "I am Miguel," said the man after sufficiently emptying his lungs and taking another deep breath. "I work at the Immigration Post. I have a note for Señor Panzer."

"How is it that you know *my* name?" Woodson asked suspiciously.

"The large one at the bus stop told me," replied Miguel pointing in the direction that he had just come.

"Oh. Why didn't *he* tell you Panzer wasn't here?"

"I asked him, but he just grunted."

"I understand."

"Could you please give this note to Señor Panzer?" he asked, holding the small scrap of paper out to Woodson.

"Is it from you?"

"No. It was left at my office last night."

"By who?"

The small man shrugged his shoulders and handed the note to Woodson.

"Gracias, Señor Woodson," said Miguel. He turned and headed back in the direction of the bus stop.

Without giving it another thought, Woodson stuffed the folded piece of paper into his pocket and followed Miguel toward the stop. The bus had just arrived as Woodson pulled up next to Hernándo. Dust billowed over the bus stop like a thick, hazy cloud as the big yellow bus finally came to a complete stop.

This truly was a chicken bus. An old converted school bus that looked as if it were at least thirty years old. The side of the bus covered by rust and spray-painted graffiti, nearly blended with windows, so thickly covered with dirt and grit from the jungle highway that it was nearly impossible to see through them.

One by one, the two and four legged occupants of the bus filed out onto the dusty road. Finally, Woodson spied a familiar face as the old man step gingerly to the ground. It was Keh. The old shaman looked cautiously toward Woodson and Hernándo. As Hernándo reached to help Keh with his bag, the old shaman pulled it away and shook his head.

"What is wrong, old man? Am I not good enough to take your bag?" Hernándo asked sarcastically. "I will not steal from you!"

Keh stared deeply into the large Mayan's eyes and said coldly, "I possess nothing that any man could want, even you, my large friend!"

"What does that mean?" Hernándo glared at the shaman. "You do not even know me."

"It means what you want it to mean," replied Keh. "I control no man's thoughts."

Woodson figured that it might be a good time to step in and separate these two.

"Keh, good to see you my new friend," he said. Woodson stepped between the Mayans.

"Ah, Señor Woodson," replied Keh with a pleasant smile. "You are looking much better today then you did the last time we met."

Hernándo turned and stormed off toward the car. Keh grabbed Woodson's arm and pulled him close.

"This one has evil in him," he warned softly. "You must be careful. Do you understand?"

CHAPTER EIGHT
The Plan

"What do you think they're doing out here, Smith?" asked Franz, looking away to protect his eyes from the sparks while stirring the campfire with a long stick.

"I'm not sure, Franz," replied Smith. "Maybe they are simply what they appear to be, archeologists. Who knows?" Smith stroked his close-cropped beard. "But, why is Panzer with them? He's a collector."

Smith stood up and looked around. Except for a few clouds that hung just above the trees, the sky had cleared. The west was ablaze with bright orange as the evening sun signaled the end of another day.

"It should be a beautiful day tomorrow," said Smith as he observed the brilliant sunset. "Where *is* Hans with that tequila?" he snapped. "He should have been back hours ago."

"Hans has always been a little slow, my friend," replied Franz. He continued to stoke the now roaring fire. "Relax, he'll be here soon." Franz started to laugh. "Remember, he's a sailor. He doesn't do well on land, eh?" he said with a snort. "By the way, what was in that note that you left for Panzer?"

"I just want him to know that I'm close by if he should need my services," began Smith. "I told him that I had heard that he was down here and that I was an archeologist who would love to meet him." Now Smith was laughing. "This way, I can be close and not cause any suspicion. I mean, we need to take care of one of our best customers. Don't we, Franz?"

"What does that mean?" Franz shot Smith a questioning glance.

"What it means, my friend, is that without Panzer, and others like him, we have no market for those delightful little artifacts that your trusted ship takes to Europe. That's what it means!"

"But Smith... what are we to do now? If we follow them, they will surely find it suspicious." Franz looked concerned. "What *if* they stumble onto the site?" he asked. "That could put us out of business!"

Smith looked into the fire and laughed. It was a wicked, hollow laugh. It made the hair on Franz's arms and neck stand on end.

"Franz, I thought you knew me better than that," he replied sarcastically. Then turning dead serious said, "I don't take any chances. One of my chicleros is with them now. He will let me know what they're up to." A small, flaming piece of wood rolled away from the fire. Smith walked over and kicked the glowing coal back into the flames. "Anyway I think I have a workable plan. If we scare them enough, I think we can have them eating right out of our hands. Hey, you and your friend Hans agreed to come with me. You wanted to see the site where the stelae come from, so let *me* do the thinking. This is my turf and I know what I'm doing." Smith looked around impatiently. "Where *is* Hans? I could really use a drink!"

Woodson stood at the edge of the camp admiring the skies' reddish orange glow as the sun set lazily over the jungle. Lost in thought, he did not notice Carla strolling up behind him.

"Beautiful, isn't it?" she said softly.

Woodson turned with a start. "Why, yes, Carla... I mean Ms. Jamison," he said awkwardly. "It is quite a sunset."

"What's with the 'Ms. Jamison' stuff? Please, call me Carla."

"Okay... Ms. Jamison...I mean Carla."

"It's your girlfriend, isn't it?" asked Carla. "I think she might be jealous."

"Look, Ms. Ja... I mean, Carla," replied Woodson, "You have to understand that Blue and I go back a long way. Some time ago, she drifted out of my life. A few months ago, we found each other again. Maybe she's just going through a period of adjustment."

"I see. Another woman just kind of complicates matters, right?"

"Exactly!" Woodson felt sweat forming uncomfortably on his brow as he spoke.

Woodson and Carla stood in silence watching the day gracefully fade into night. After the sun had set, they walked back to camp. Neither Woodson nor Carla spoke. Woodson sensed the tension. He was sure that Carla was attracted to him. Woodson was also certain that Blue would not appreciate Carla's attention toward him. There had to be a way for these two women to get along on this trip. He just had to think of how. When they had reached Carla's tent, he broke the uncomfortable silence.

"Look, Carla. I think it would be a good idea if you tried to know Blue a little better. It might ease some of the tension between—"

Just then, he heard a familiar voice from behind.

"Where have you been, Woody?" inquired Blue, glaring at Carla.

"Hi, Blue," Woodson felt the blood rush to his face. "Ms. Jamison and I were just admiring the sunset. I hope you didn't miss it."

Blue sauntered up to the pair. She was not quite sure how to read what was going on.

"Thanks for keeping an eye on this one for me, Ms. Jamison," she said with a chuckle. "No telling what trouble he'll get into when I'm not around."

Woodson winced at her comment. He was sure that Blue was about to erupt at any second.

"No problem," replied Carla, with a smile. "May I call you Blue?

"Sure, why not."

"You know, Blue," began Carla, glancing at Blue's attire, "I couldn't help noticing your field wear. They look so comfortable, and they fit you so well."

"Why thank you, Ms. Jamison."

"Please! Call me Carla."

"Why thank you, Carla."

Woodson, uncertain where this was going, decided it best to interrupt. "Blue."

"You know Carla," said Blue, "I might just have something that will fit you." Blue reached over and rubbed the material of Carla's shirt between her fingers. "It would be so much better in this heat than what you're wearing."

"Oh, that would be great," replied Carla. "I've never been in the jungle before."

"Blue... Carla," said Woodson, trying to get their attention.

"C'mon Carla, let's go to my tent," said Blue. The two women walked away talking like old school mates.

Woodson stood there in disbelief. "Well, that was easy." he said to himself pretending to wipe dust from his hands.

Woodson stood quietly outside of Panzer's tent. He knew that he had forgotten something, but he just could not remember what it was. Then, reaching absent-mindedly into his pocket, his fingers felt the folded scrap of paper that the little man from the Immigration Post had given him in El Naranjo. *That's it,* he thought. Between keeping the two Mayans apart at the train station, his run-in with Carla, and the beautiful sunset, Woodson had been so distracted that he had forgotten all about the note for Panzer. He slapped at the tent and called out to Panzer.

"Mr. Panzer? Jon? Are you there?"

"Come in." replied Panzer impatiently.

Woodson pulled the flap away and squeezed through the narrow opening. In the center of the dimly lit tent, Panzer and Hernándo stood bent over a large sheet of tracing paper that draped stiffly over the sides of a small rectangular case. Panzer held a flashlight directly over the tracing, casting a round, concentrated glow of light onto the center. Woodson recognized the familiar squared shapes of ancient Mayan glyphs that filled the sheet. Panzer looked up to see who had entered the tent.

"Ah! Woody," he said with great satisfaction. "Just the man I wanted to see!" Panzer handed the flashlight to the archeologist. "Here, take a look at this and tell me what you make of it."

Woodson knelt down next to Panzer and eyed the penciled tracings. After a few moments of intense study, he turned toward Panzer. Woodson's broad smile of satisfaction betrayed his apparent excitement.

"Where did you get this?" he inquired in disbelief.

"I *thought* you might find it interesting," replied Panzer, unable to hide his delight. "Hernándo went to scout our route to the river and found a small group of buildings hidden in the jungle. The stele from which this tracing was taken stands at the center of this group of buildings."

"Nice tracing job, Hernándo," said Woodson. "Couldn't have done it better myself."

Hernándo grunted.

"Can you read it?" Panzer inquired. "This could have something to do with the lost city!"

"I think so," Woodson said thoughtfully. "Got a better flashlight?"

Panzer rummaged through his backpack and handed Woodson a large long-handled flashlight.

"This should do," he said. Woodson took the light from Panzer. "Give me a couple minutes. I'll be right outside."

Woodson carefully folded the tracing and slipped out of the tent. Looking around he noticed a large flat rock that was no more than ten feet away. "That should do nicely," he said to himself and he made for the rock. Woodson started translating the tracing before he even reached the rock. Not paying attention to where he was walking, carelessly, he almost tripped over it. Finally, seated and flashlight in place, Woodson began his work.

The way to this place has not been easy. My father has died. I, his eldest son, now lead our people. We have come so far and withstood such hardship. The people are sad to have left their birthplace and sacred homeland. But, they still live and that was my father's dying wish. Our heritage and our way of life must survive.

This place is our new home for now. We found this abandoned village. The people who had built this place appear to have been very much like our own. The construction is much the same way as we build our temples.

We are close to the river of which my father spoke. I pray that we soon find our final home.

Satisfied with his work, Woodson slipped back into Panzer's tent and handed him the translation.

"Looks like we're on the right track, Panzer," he said. "This stele obviously chronicles a journey. They're the words of the eldest son of the group's leader." Woodson shook his head. "I find it hard to believe, but this might just be what you're looking for."

Panzer took Woodson's scribbled translation and placed it carefully on the trunk. Woodson observed the excitement on the collector's face as he ran his flashlight over the translations. Then glancing over at Hernándo, Woodson noticed that the large Mayan appeared more than a little uncomfortable.

Panzer looked up quickly to get Woodson's attention.

"This is fantastic, Woody," he said with great delight. "What a stroke of luck. This proves that the map on the pottery shard is the real deal—"

"Speaking of that shard," Woodson interrupted. "I wonder if you might let me take another look at it, I might pick up on some things that you could have missed."

Panzer reached over, picked up a small leather bag, and handed it to Woodson. "I don't have to tell *you* how fragile it is," warned Panzer, "please be careful."

Woodson took the small bag. Just as he was about to open it to look at the shard, something jogged his memory.

"Oh, by the way, Jon," he said, reaching deeply into the pocket of his jeans. "I forgot to give this to you. A man from the Immigration Post told me that somebody had left it for you."

Panzer eagerly unfolded the small piece of paper. As he read, his face showed concern. His mood changed noticeably.

"Take a look at this, Woody."

Woodson read the note before exclaiming, "Smith!"

Panzer stood up, took the note back, and read it again.

"It seems that our Mr. Smith is unaware that we're on to who he really is. He's trying to make us think that he's a fellow archeologist." Panzer looked to Woodson. "What do you think we should do, Woody? You're in charge!"

"I think we should play along with this joker," he replied. "If he says that he's an archeologist, then let's treat him like one." Woodson snatched the note from Panzer's hand and waved it in the air. "This way," he continued, "when we meet face-to-face, he'll think that we're still in the dark about who he really is. You're sure *he's the guy* who is robbing Site Q?"

"To the best of my knowledge, Dennis Smith *is* the smuggler's name."

Woodson looked over at Hernándo.

"You sure are being quiet. No opinion on this?"

Hernándo shook his head.

"I work for Mr. Panzer," replied the large Mayan. "What he thinks is all that matters. Now, if you will excuse me, I think it is time to get some rest."

"You may work for Mr. Panzer," Woodson said with a distinct air of authority, "but I was hired to lead this expedition! So if you wouldn't mind, I sure would like to see the village where you found the stele."

"Maybe tomorrow," snapped Hernando, before leaving the tent.

"How well do you know this Hernándo character, Jon?" asked Woodson once the Mayan had gone.

"I just met him in person when you did," he replied. "We've been in phone contact for a while. I hired him to set things up before we arrived. The archeologist who found the shard that you have there in your hand, referred Hernándo. Why?"

"I just don't trust him," said Woodson thoughtfully. "Keh doesn't either."

"You just met Keh a couple of days ago. How can you be certain about him?"

"If my friend Angel says he's okay," replied Woodson, "then he's okay in my book. I would trust Angel with my life."

"If you trust him so much, why didn't you bring Angel instead of Keh?"

"Angel is retiring soon. He has to train his replacement, and just couldn't get away." Woodson held up the small leather bag that contained the mysterious pottery shard. "Look, I'm going to go over this shard with Lyons and Pedro. If we find anything important, I'll let you know. In the meantime, let us see if we can meet up with this person Smith. Before we head out in the morning, see if you can get a note to our little friend, Miguel at the Immigration Office, maybe he can get it to Smith."

"What should it say?" inquired Panzer.

"Tell him that we're headed toward the Usamacinta River—"

Before Woodson could finish, there was a loud explosion. Without another word, he and Panzer bolted from the tent. Noise and commotion filled the air; the camp was in a complete panic. Blue and Carla ran in the direction of Panzer's tent at full speed.

"Woody! Woody! What's happening?" shouted Blue. "What was that—?"

Another explosion rocked the small camp. This time, it sounded much closer. Woodson grabbed both Blue and Carla by the arm and pushed them through the small opening in Panzer's tent.

"Stay here and keep your heads down!" he exclaimed.

Blue's head immediately popped back out of the tent.

"What's going on?" she cried.

"Sounds like rifle fire, Blue!" he replied, gently pushing her head back into the tent. "Now, stay here. I'll be back! Panzer, come with me! I—" There was another loud blast. This time, Woodson knew exactly what it was. "Shotgun!" yelled Woodson. He grabbed Panzer and pulled him to the ground.

"Who could be shooting at us?" cried Panzer nervously.

"Dunno," replied Woodson, before turning toward the center of the camp. *"Pedro!"* he shouted upon spotting his young assistant and Professor Lyons leaping wildly over the campfire making for the cover of one of the Jeeps.

"My bow, Pedro, get my bow! It's in the tent right behind you!" cried Woodson. Another shot filled the air. *"Get my bow!"*

Pedro pushed Lyons down next to one of the Jeeps before quickly ducking into the opening in Woodson's tent. Another blast echoed through the once still night. Closer! Woodson leaped over the Jeep to check on the professor.

"Lyons! Are you okay?" he cried.

Lyons looked up at Woodson, smiled, and reached under his jacket. The professor pulled out a small, black handgun.

"What in the world is that?" cried Woodson upon seeing the weapon. "You never told me you were armed!"

"You never asked!" replied Lyons.

The shots were coming one after the other, from three different directions. Pedro, with Woodson's case in hand, suddenly appeared out of nowhere.

"Thanks kid," he said. Woodson quickly opened the case and removed the bow. He carefully strung his bow and pulled one of the long sleek arrows from its quiver. "Can anyone see where the shots are coming from?" he cried. "Panzer, are you okay?"

Panzer crawled up from behind the Jeep.

"I'm here, Woody."

"You got a gun?"

"Are you kidding?" Panzer cried incredulously. "This is the *last thing* I expected!"

Three more shots rang out. The pellets from the blasts made a ticking sound as they rapidly skidded across the ground around them.

"We're sitting ducks here!" exclaimed Woodson. "We'd better split up!"

"Woody, look!" screamed Pedro, pointing toward the campfire at the center of the camp.

Keh's shadowy figure appeared before the fire. The old shaman was shouting something, but neither Woodson nor Pedro could make it out. The old man kept pointing toward a specific area in the jungle that was directly in line with the front of the Jeep. Pedro suddenly understood what the old man was doing.

Like a cat, young Pedro jumped into the open vehicle and flipped on the headlights. Just as they came on, there was another shot and Keh slumped to the ground. Now visible, just beyond the fallen Keh was the shadowy figure of a large man. Jumping to his feet, Woodson pulled his bow tight and took careful aim at the shadow. Sweat poured from his brow, he felt his fingers tense against the taught bowstring. The shadowy figure began to move, but it was too late. Woodson's target was now securely in his sight. He let the arrow fly. A couple of long, agonizing seconds passed before the shadowy figure cried out in pain.

"I've been hit!" cried the voice

Woodson pulled another arrow from the case and headed towards Keh at a full run. When he arrived at the spot where Keh had fallen, he found bloodstains on the old man's shirt.

"Are you all right?" Woodson shouted.

Keh sat up. Woodson could see the pain in the deeply cut features. Keh grabbed his bleeding shoulder.

"I am fine, my young friend," the old shaman gasped. "Go! Catch the ones who did this!"

Woodson took a quick look at the wound and yelled out to his friends. "Pedro! Look after Keh. See if you can stop the bleeding. Professor, come with me!"

Woodson and Lyons rushed ahead to the spot where they had seen the attacker go down, but he was gone. Lyons dropped to one knee and inspected the ground. Woodson walked around slashing at the brush with his bow.

"Woody—blood!" Lyons called out.

Woodson rushed over.

"Over there, Professor, someone was dragged away... that way!" he said, pointing to where the clearing ended.

"Should we go after them?"

"No," Woodson replied sharply. "We have no idea how many shooters there were. We'd better get back to camp."

The large sailor fell to the ground struggling to catch his breath.

"Great idea, Smith!" exclaimed Hans, through clinched teeth. "We scared them, all right! Look at my leg! That arrow went clean through it. It really hurts!" he cried, as he lay writhing in pain.

"Relax! I'll have that out in a jiffy," Smith snapped. He knelt down and pulled a large, shiny, hunting knife from his belt.

"What do you care?" Hans snapped back. "It's not sticking out of *your* leg!"

Smith grabbed the tipped end of the arrow that had exited Hans' right calf and with a strong jerk, cut it off.

"Ow!" exclaimed Hans. "What are you doing—?"

"I just cut the tip off the arrow," replied Smith. "Hold on! I'm gonna pull it out."

"*Franz!*"

"What, Hans?"

"*I think I need something to bite on!*"

Smith pulled what was left of the arrow smoothly from Hans' leg. Quickly, he applied a compress to the wound to stop the bleeding

"Hans, are you okay? Hans?" asked Franz, gently slapping at Hans' face.

"He passed right out, Franz," observed Smith calmly. "Usually happens with that much pain."

"Is he going to be okay?"

"Sure, this big ox is too dumb to die," replied Smith. He inspected the arrow shaft before tossing it carelessly into the nearby brush.

Smith poured two tequilas and handed one to Franz. For a few minutes, the two men sat in silence sipping their drinks. Occasionally, they would glance to see how their fallen companion fared.

"Some plan," said Franz, breaking the uncomfortable silence. "I thought we were just going to put a little scare into them. Why all the drama? We might have killed somebody back there!"

"Look!" replied Smith stiffly, growing impatient listening to Franz's questions. "I figured if they thought there were banditos around here, they might turn back. I didn't plan for anyone to get hurt—*yet.*"

Smith downed the rest of his tequila and sat motionless by the fire. He neither moved nor spoke until the first light of dawn.

CHAPTER NINE
Nawal

It was just before dawn. A misty gray sky hung heavily over the embattled camp. Woodson had volunteered to take the last watch while the others tried to get some sleep. The events of the night had put everyone on edge; most were still awake and stirring nervously in their tents. Approaching Keh's tent, Woodson decided that this would probably be a good time to check in on the wounded shaman. Standing near the tent's opening; Woodson hesitated before calling out. He heard the muffled sound of the old man chanting inside. Not wanting to disturb Keh's privacy, Woodson turned away.

"Come in my young friend," said the raspy voice from within. "I have been expecting you."

Woodson turned, pulled away the flap, and stepped through the narrow opening. The shadowy figure of Keh sat cross-legged at the center of the tent. A small pot of incense sat smoking before him. The tent, so dimly lit by a small lantern that Woodson could barely make out the thin, soft ribbon of smoke that rose from the pot into the air.

"Come, sit down, Professor," said the old man. "You are welcome." Keh motioned to a small rug directly across from his.

Woodson joined the old shaman on the tent floor.

"How's that shoulder doing?" he asked.

The old man placed a knurled hand on his bandaged shoulder and gave it a gentle rub.

"I will live," he said smiling. "It will take more than a few small pieces of lead for *this* old man to join his ancestors at *the shrine*."

Woodson smiled and leaned over to inspect Keh's bandaged wound.

"It looks okay," he said reassuringly. "I think we got all the lead out." Woodson settled back onto the rug and scratched at his two-day-old stubble. "What shrine are you talking about?" he inquired.

The old man moved his hand over the burning incense. The smoke looked like small snakes escaping between his fingers. Slowly, he looked up at Woodson and smiled.

"The Quiché Maya believe that when great shamans die, as I will some day," began Keh, his voice was soft, and low, "their souls meet at the family shrine, the place where they worshiped during their time in this world. As the years go by, many souls gather at this shrine, giving it great power. We call this shrine *warabálja.*"

"Sleeping places!" exclaimed Woodson, before realizing that he had interrupted Keh. "Sorry."

"Do you know the rest, my young friend?" asked Keh, sounding very impressed that Woodson possessed the knowledge of his people.

"I think so," he replied sheepishly, hoping not to offend the old shaman.

"You know much about my people, yes?" Keh smiled. He already knew the answer.

"I find Maya culture fascinating," replied the now animated Woodson. He lived for Maya culture. He could never learn enough about their ancient ways. "I have devoted my entire career to it!" Woodson stated proudly.

The old man leaned forward. "Do your companions know?" he whispered.

"Know what?"

"About your previous life," replied Keh.

"*What?*"

"You really have no idea why you love my people and their history, do you?"

Woodson stared skeptically at the old man, but uttered not a word. The silence seemed to go on forever.

"You mean the visions," he said, now certain to what Keh referred. "Angel told you about my visions, didn't he?"

Keh leaned over the incense and sniffed noisily at the thin plume of smoke. Then, he growled, *"Those were not visions!"*

Goose bumps popped up on Woodson's arms.

Keh began the ancient chants for the second time in the last few days. Woodson suddenly felt weak, almost faint. The old man appeared to be spinning wildly around Woodson's reeling head. Keh continued to chant in ancient Mayan, but the phrases were unfamiliar, far more ancient than Woodson had ever heard before.

Now the entire tent and all its belongings were spinning around Woodson as if he sat in the eye of a tiny hurricane. He was beginning to lose control. Keh had nearly spun to a blur when Woodson felt a cool wind blow through the tent. Again, just as he did on that day at the mouth of the cave when he first met Keh, he could sense the fresh cleansing air filling his eager nostrils. The cool, refreshing wind blew through the tent and joined the swirling winds. Woodson was certain that he was going mad. Then suddenly, it all stopped. Everything was back to normal. Still reeling from the experience, Woodson shook his head, in disbelief. He felt confused and disorientated. Woodson's hands shook nervously; he looked to Keh for answers.

"Did you feel that?" Woodson asked, finally able to gather up his wits.

"Feel what, my young friend," Keh replied.

"You were spinning around the tent..." Woodson rubbed his eyes, still in disbelief. "The entire tent was spinning around my head," he said softly. His hands trembled. "Am I going mad?"

The old shaman shook his head and smiled.

"The spirits within you are gaining strength, Professor."

"You, too?" cried Woodson. "Angel told me the same thing. Is it Guerrero?"

Keh shook his head again. He replied softly, "Do not question who or what they may be, all will be made clear."

"When?" inquired Woodson.

"That will be up to the spirit," Keh replied. "When the time comes, the spirit will reveal itself to you."

"But Keh—" Woodson was interrupted by the familiar sound of Blue's voice.

"Woody! Where are you?" said Blue. She was just outside Keh's tent.

Woodson struggled to his feet.

"I'm here, Blue, I'll be right out," he said loudly. Woodson smiled at the old shaman, he was feeling under control again. More like his old self. "You need some help packing up?"

"I think I can handle it. My shoulder is good," replied Keh

Woodson had started to open the tent flap when he paused to look back at Keh. "Will you or Angel ever be able to explain what has happened to me?"

"In time, Professor Woodson," whispered Keh, "all will be known to you and the other."

"You mean, Pedro?"

"You know?" Keh seemed surprised. "The spirits are strong in the young one as well, Professor."

Woodson let out a long sigh and shrugged his shoulders. *Angel was right*, he thought, before exiting the tent. He was halfway through the narrow opening then stopped. Woodson pulled back into the tent.

"My friends call me Woody," he said softly.

"Then, I shall call you Woody as well," replied Keh.

Woodson gave the old shaman a wink before squeezing through the narrow opening.

By the time the sun had risen above the jungle's tall trees, the Jeeps were loaded and the expedition started out for the river. Woodson pulled his Jeep in line behind Panzer's cutting a rugged path through the dense jungle. Hernándo sat at the wheel of the lead Jeep driving incredibly fast for the bumpy, overgrown terrain. Keh, who sat in the back seat of Hernándo's Jeep, held his wounded shoulder tightly. He and Carla nearly bounced off the seat with every bump.

"What's Hernándo doing?" cried Woodson, struggling to keep the jeep from veering off into the thick jungle. "He's going to get us all killed!"

Pedro held out a small two-way radio. "Here Woody, here's the radio. Call him!"

"Hernándo, what's the hurry?" cried Woodson. He jerked the wheel to the right just missing an old stump jutting out from the old dirt and grass road. "You're going *way* to fast. Watch out! Geez, you almost hit that tree!"

"I thought you were in a hurry to see the stele, Señor?" replied Hernándo, laughing.

"It's been there for almost a thousand years," cried Woodson. "I don't think it's going anywhere. *Now, slow down!*"

Woodson took a deep sigh of relief as Hernándo's vehicle slowed. Low, leaf-filled branches and stringy vines had begun to obstruct the tiny road making it nearly impossible to see the other Jeep.

"Good thing we slowed down," said Pedro. "I can't see a thing."

"What do you think that was all about," asked Blue.

Woodson slowed the Jeep to a crawl to prevent them from being slashed by the encroaching branches. "I'm not sure. But I aim to find out," he replied angrily.

Hernándo slowed the lead car to a stop and motioned out toward the jungle. Woodson pulled in just behind. He jumped out and struggled through the thick brush that lined the narrow path toward Hernándo.

"Here we are, Señor Woodson," said Hernándo motioning into the jungle. "This path leads to the little village and your stele."

"Never mind that, Hernándo," began Woodson angrily, "What was that all about?"

"Que?"

"Don't give me that—"

"I didn't mean to scare you, Professor Woodson," snapped Hernándo.

"Just remember who's in charge here!" exclaimed Woodson.

Hernándo glanced at Panzer. Panzer gave the large guide a quick nod. It did not escape Woodson's attention.

"I am sorry, Professor Woodson," Hernándo said blandly. "It will not happen again."

Woodson turned toward the jungle and spotted a freshly trodden path.

"That's better," he said, before pointing down the path. "How far is it to the stele?"

"Not far," replied Hernándo. "Come, I will show you."

With Hernándo in the lead, the group started down the dew-moistened path. The vine-laden jungle was so dense that the sun was barely able to break through the trees. The footing was unsure and Keh struggled trying to navigate the slippery path. Pedro took Keh by the arm and helped him through the damp brush. The old shaman smiled appreciatively watching young Pedro push away thick branches and hanging obstructions to clear the way.

Soon, the narrow, winding path widened into a small clearing. The morning light poured over the area revealing three tiny, gray-stone buildings built around a small square, or common area. It was obvious the jungle had reclaimed the small village. It was equally apparent by the hastily cleared square, that someone had recently been there—someone other than Hernándo.

As they drew closer to the small cleared area, they easily spotted the stele. Small, but still standing straight, the limestone pillar stood about three feet above the surrounding brush.

"This is amazing!" Woodson exclaimed. "I can't believe this stele has escaped the chicleros. Somebody has definitely cleared this site. The buildings seem far too clear of jungle growth."

Lyons and Panzer were first to reach the stele. Each quickly inspected the carvings while Woodson and Pedro took pictures of the buildings that surrounded the square.

Woodson felt a stiff chill run down his spine. The hairs on his arms suddenly stood straight up. Then another icy coolness ran down Woodson's back. He looked at Pedro. The young man's eyes were the size of saucers. The sound of someone softly chanting filled the still jungle air. It was Keh. The old man closed his eyes and cried out to the Gods.

"Woody! Something is wrong with Keh!" cried Pedro.

Woodson quickly pulled himself together and ran to Keh's side.

"What is it, Keh?" he asked.

Keh did not respond. He opened his eyes slowly glancing around the small village.

Pedro joined Woodson.

"This place gives me the creeps," he said nervously.

"Me too," he replied. Woodson turned to Keh. "What is it?"

"There is evil here, Professor! We must leave at once!" He finally replied. Keh's dark, wrinkled face had turned an ashen gray.

"What do you see?" asked Pedro, now peering suspiciously around the small village.

"There!" cried the old shaman, pointing toward the stele. "You cannot see them, but they *are* there!"

"Who?" asked Woodson, looking directly into Keh's eyes. "Tell us, what do you see?"

"*Nawal!*" replied Keh. The old man pointed repeatedly toward the stele. "They are the spirits of the many who died here long ago! There was great shame here—so many had to die! The *nawal,* Woody, can you not see them. They are everywhere!"

"Okay! Now I officially have the creeps," said Blue, with a shudder.

"We must leave here...now," pleaded Keh. "We must go to the river! We must go to the river"

"Pedro." Woodson turned to his young assistant. "Take Keh back to the Jeep. Blue, you, and Carla go with them." Woodson tossed the camera to Lyons. "Professor, take the camera and finish the roll on those buildings over there. Panzer, you come with me. We need to see if Hernándo missed any glyphs on the stele. Hurry up people; I think it might be a good idea to get out of here

Hernándo grabbed Woodson's arm and spun him around.

"You listen to the old one?" he growled.

"Yes," replied Woodson. He glared with narrowed eyes at Hernándo's hand upon his arm. The guide immediately released his grip.

"Why?" Hernándo protested. "He is an old fool. You cannot take him seriously."

"We are moving out *ASAP!*" exclaimed Woodson impatiently. "Your job is to get us to the river. *Got it?* Now, let's move out!"

"What's a *nawal*?" asked Panzer.

"*Nawal* are souls," began Woodson, "the Maya believe they are the souls of their dead ancestors."

"Keh saw the spirit of his ancestors here?" inquired Panzer incredulously

"Look," began Woodson. He paused briefly to gather his thoughts. "Keh is a shaman, or holy man. Shamans have special powers. If the conditions are right, they can see the ancestors of their people, the Maya. I can't explain it, but if it scared him, then I'm for getting as far away from this place as possible!"

As Woodson and Panzer examined the stele, they heard a shout from the other side of the village. It was Lyons.

"Woody! You'd better get over here."

Woodson ran across the small compound with Panzer close on his heels. When they arrived, they found Lyons standing over a small fire-blackened altar made from a large circular flat stone. Only three feet above the ground, the altar's smooth, flat surface appeared coated with melted, white candle wax. At each of the four cardinal points of the compass were small, nearly spent candles. Woodson bent over the altar to get a closer look. Stained onto the fire-blackened surface of the stone was a deep brownish-red.

"So that's why the chicleros haven't sold this place off," he said.

"I get it," said Lyons, eying the altar. "They're using it as a holy place, a place of sacrifice."

"Right, Professor," replied Woodson. He rubbed the brownish red substance that covered the altar.

Blood?" asked Lyons. His voice trembled as he spoke the word, his face completely drained of color.

"I'm afraid so, Professor," replied Woodson. "Look! There are feathers scattered about. Somebody sacrificed a chicken here and it wasn't all that long ago." Woodson pointed at the four nearly spent piles of wax. "Those candles mark the four cardinal points of the compass and the wax still feels warm." Then he reached over and picked up a large shard of pottery. "Codex!" he exclaimed.

"That's impossible," said Lyons.

"Why?" stated Woodson. "This site has obviously been overlooked by archeologists."

"Then who cleared it?"

"The chicleros," replied Woodson, still staring at the small altar of death. "Who else could it have been? Finish taking your pictures and head back. Get me a few angles on this altar, as well." Woodson pointed at the buildings. "Here. Throw this piece of pottery in your bag. We can look at it later. I'll stay here until everyone is safely on the path back to the Jeeps. Now let's go!"

Once Lyons and the others had made it to the path safely, Woodson took one last look at the small village. He wondered what Keh had seen and how the spirits might have appeared. Woodson and Pedro had felt their presence as well. His mind turned to Guerrero again. As Woodson left to join the others, a dark figure stepped out from the shadow of the tiny buildings. It was Dennis Smith.

"You can come out now, Franz. They've gone."

Franz emerged from the thick brush of the jungle.

"Now what?" asked Franz. Hurriedly he brushed at thick spider webs that clung annoyingly to his shirt.

"We head for the river, that's what!"

"Why?"

"Why? Because, Franz, the time has come to introduce myself to the esteemed Professor Woodson and his party, don't you think?"

CHAPTER TEN
The River

"How much farther, Woody?" yelled Blue from the backseat of the Jeep.

Though he could hear her, Woodson hesitated to answer. The narrow jungle path they were traveling was extremely difficult to navigate. Brush and trees lurked around every corner and, at that moment, driving needed all his attention.

"Shouldn't be too far ahead," he replied, once the terrain had improved and driving did not require his full attention. "Pedro, you've got the map. What do you think?"

"According to the map," replied Pedro, the wind slapping the thin paper map against his tanned face, "We should be there soon. It can't be more than a few miles away."

Blue pulled herself between the two front seats. Her long brown hair flapped wildly in the wind and she struggled to keep it out of her eyes.

"So what's the deal on this river?" she asked.

"We're going to head south on the river until we reach a bend about twenty miles north of Frontera Corozal," replied Woodson. "The map on Panzer's pottery shard indicated that as the area we need to search."

"Why didn't we just go there *directly* instead of the long way around?" Blue inquired, finally getting control of her windblown hair.

"Good question," began Woodson. "Even though Frontera Corozal is on the Mexican side of the river, we thought it might be smarter to avoid getting too close. Hernándo said there were many looters in the area. I figured it might be dangerous if too many people knew we were here."

"Woody! The river!" exclaimed Pedro, pointing straight ahead.

As they approached a clearing, it became apparent that the path turned sharply to run alongside the river. The densely treed jungle had given way to low-lying brush that grew right up to the edge of the yellowish, brown water of the great Usumacinta River. Now heading south, they could clearly see the river gently snaking its way along the Mexican and Guatemalan border.

"Not very pretty, Woody," observed Blue. "That's one dirty-looking river."

"I know," he replied sadly. "I expected a lot more from the river that was one of the most important trade routes of the ancient Maya."

Woodson grabbed the two-way radio.

"Hernándo," Woodson shouted into the small radio. "How long before we reach the campsite?"

The answer came back immediately, Hernándo's voice crackling through the radio's static.

"Just up ahead, Señor Woodson, below that large tree that hangs over the river."

There was a fair amount of activity on the river that day. The Usamacinta River was still used quite extensively for trade and travel. Whether it was to ship their crops, goods, or fish, many of the local Guatemalans and Mexicans made their living from the river. Woodson was well aware of this river's importance to the local culture and that they must be very careful not to interrupt regular activities. The people on the river do eventually arrive in towns and villages. Woodson figured the fewer people that knew about this expedition, the better.

As they pulled up to the campsite, Woodson noticed someone waving toward the river. It was Keh. He watched as Keh pointed toward the opposite side of the river. There,

Woodson saw a mother and two small children as they made their way down river in a small, ancient-looking dugout canoe. The little ones were girls dressed in *huipiles*; brightly colored, long, sleeveless tunics. The two girls, who could not have been much older than six or seven years old, wore equally colorful woven, tasseled hats that the Maya call *tocoyal.* They smiled and waved wildly at the old shaman. Woodson could not help but notice the broad smile on Keh's face when he waved back. As the Jeep came to a stop, Blue jumped out to get a better look.

"They are adorable," she said, when she reached the old shaman. "What lovely outfits. Keh, can tell me about the people here?"

Keh took Blue by the hand and said, "Listen, when I tell you that what we come here to find means nothing. These children, they mean everything."

Blue looked into Keh's eyes, then back toward the children and smiled.

The next morning, as they broke camp, Woodson and Pedro walked down to the river's bank. The morning was quiet, except for the occasional call of the wild birds that flew playfully from tree to tree. The birds were curious about the presence of these noisy humans.

Woodson looked up river. There were two distant objects headed their way.

What time is it, Pedro?" asked Woodson, still looking up river.

"Seven forty-five, Woody," he replied.

"The boats are right on time," said Woodson. "You'd better go tell everybody."

Pedro turned and headed back to camp.

"Okay, people," he said loudly. "The boats are coming. Woody said to get going."

Hernándo passed Pedro then started down the hill toward the river. Woodson pointed toward the two boats.

"Pretty big boats, Hernándo," said Woodson, once the guide arrived at the river's edge.

"Si, they are big enough," he replied.

"They look like the boats your ancestors rode this river in."

"Si. For a thousand years, the Maya used this river to carry cacao, jade, and jaguar skins to be traded in the great cities of the North."

"Your people accomplished great things, Hernándo," Woodson said softly. "You should be proud."

Hernándo stared at the approaching boats.

"Professor," he said after a long silence. "Why do you seek this lost city? Will this make you rich?"

"No, I'm afraid not," replied Woodson shaking his head. "We're here to discover another piece of your past— your history."

"But, Panzer pays you. Does he not?" Hernándo inquired suspiciously. "He pays me!"

"Yes, he does. But, I would be here even if he didn't."

"You really care about my people."

"Yes. Yes, I do!"

The large Mayan looked back toward the river. Without looking back he said, "The boats are almost here. I will give Pedro a hand with the gear."

As Hernándo walked away, Woodson could not help but feel that he had made some kind of connection with the large Mayan. He still suspected that Hernándo was acting on Smith's orders. Now, Woodson felt the Mayan was feeling confused and unsure. He hoped that this would work to his advantage.

"Okay. I want Hernándo, Panzer, Lyons, and Carla in the first boat," shouted Woodson, loading his bags into the second boat. "Do you hombres speak English?" he asked the two boatmen.

The taller of the two men spoke first. "Enough, I think," he growled, watching Woodson, Pedro and Hernándo load the gear into the boats.

"What are your names?" inquired Pedro.

"I am Lopez," he said proudly, "and this is my brother, Miguel. But we call him, Que."

"Que, isn't that Maya for parrot?"

"Si, my brother repeats anything you say to him," volunteered Lopez.

"I see," said Pedro. "Well, Lopez, Que, its great meeting you—"

"Its great meeting you—" Que quickly mimicked Pedro.

"I see what you mean," said Pedro, turning to Lopez.

"I see what you mean," said Que, mimicking Pedro again.

"This is not going to work, boys!" exclaimed Blue who had been standing there patiently listening to this silly exchange.

Just as Que was about to speak, Blue placed her hand over Que's mouth and shook her head. Que got the message, smiled, and quietly stowed her gear on the boat.

"Nice work, Blue," whispered Lyons. "I was getting ready to shoot him." Then, extending his hand to Carla, Lyons said, "My dear, Ms. Jamison, allow me to help you into the boat" Carla gave Lyons a smile, took his hand, and carefully stepped into the wide dugout canoe. Woodson rolled his eyes and the professor shot him a mischievous smile.

The Usumacinta River was quiet that morning. The only sound heard was that of the boatman's oars as they broke the water's tranquil surface. The boat with Hernándo and Panzer took the lead. Woodson's boat followed closely in its wake. Woodson and Blue sat to the center of the small boat with Pedro and Keh just behind them.

Woodson turned to his young apprentice.

"Well Pedro, you certainly have been quiet since we started this expedition," he said with a smile.

"I haven't had much to say..." Pedro replied. He hesitated.

"C'mon, Pedro, what's the problem?" Woodson pressed the young man.

"Something isn't right here," he replied. "I'm not sure that I trust these people—Hernándo or Panzer..." Pedro hesitated again. "...I'm just a kid, but I don't think Panzer is here to preserve any ruins." Pedro shook his head. "I can tell that you don't trust Hernándo."

"You're right."

"Then, why are we here?"

"We're here because I *do* want to preserve the ruins if we find them, and you *can* be trusted." Woodson gave Pedro a light pat on the cheek. "And if I remember, it was you who got me involved in all this."

Pedro gave Woodson a big toothy grin and chuckled.

"Oh yeah, I forgot."

"That's not all, Pedro, is it?" added Keh. "Tell Woody what really bothers you, my son."

"What?" inquired Pedro. He quickly turned to face the old man.

"Tell him, Pedro," continued Keh. "Tell Woody how you are afraid that the visions will come again. Afraid that the spirits of the past are so deep within him that they follow wherever he may go. Tell him how you fear his *nawal!*"

"Is this true?" inquired Woodson.

"I think I do..." Pedro's reply was hesitant again. "...You didn't see what I saw in your eyes when you had those visions. Ask Blue. I was scared to death and so was she."

Woodson rubbed his face with both hands and sighed.

"Look Pedro, I haven't had any problems since Cozumel—"

"I think that's the problem!" Blue quickly interrupted. "We were *in* Cozumel! We were in civilization among friends. Now we're here in this jungle, with people we don't trust. I'm just as scared as Pedro."

"You should be," cried Keh. He pointed a trembling hand toward the sky. "Look!"

The wind had picked up considerably. Low, dark clouds swirled wildly just above the boats. Though it was only late morning, the sky blackened as if night had descended upon them. The boat began to roll, the river pitched and churned turning into white, foaming rapids. The river pounded against the sides of the boats. The boatmen soon lost control to the intense currents.

"Hold on, everybody!" screamed Woodson. He grabbed Blue, Pedro and Keh and pulled them down onto the bottom of the dugout. "Hold on for your lives!"

The boats swirled around and around in circles. There was no hope in controlling the helpless dugouts. A funnel formed just above causing a waterspout to explode from the raging surface. Higher and higher, it reached up into the air, filling the sky with clouds of water and misty spray.

"Not again!" screamed Blue. "This is just like Chichén Itzá!"

"*Nawals!*" yelled Keh. "They have found us!"

Woodson felt his heart sink. There was no doubt that *nawal* were there. He could feel them; they were all around—even inside. He also felt that they were there for him. *Why, why was this happening again?*

"Woody!" cried Pedro. He pointed into the air. "The spout is almost on us!" The waterspout spun closer and closer. Once over the boats, the spout launched torrents of rain with a drenching crash. Loud screeching howls reverberated through the air as the river gave one last giant heave sending the boats flying into the air. Woodson's boat came down first crashing heavily into the raging waves. It pitched and rolled, but somehow it remained afloat. The other boat was not so lucky. As it crashed back down to the surface of the water, it capsized, throwing everybody aboard splashing helplessly into the water.

Woodson and the others heard the cries of their downed companions through the roar of the howling winds, but could do nothing to help. It was nearly impossible to see through the churning mist. Woodson felt certain he could see everyone's head bobbing above the surface of the choppy brown water. Then, without warning, a whirlpool formed around those trapped in the water. Woodson felt helpless watching the rising water swirl around the tiny bobbing heads as the waterspout continued to bombard them with rain.

Woodson knew they had to do something fast before the currents sucked Lyons and the others beneath the surface.

"I'm going in!" he cried loudly so the others in the boat could hear him over the roaring winds. "Stay here, all of you, and hold on!"

Woodson grabbed a length of rope and jumped into the river. Pedro jumped in right behind him.

"What do you think you're doing?" Woodson yelled, once realizing his young apprentice had followed him into the river. "I told you to stay in the boat!"

"I go where you go!" shouted Pedro.

Woodson shook his head and shouted back, "Your grandfather will kill me if anything happens to you!" Woodson wrapped the rope around his waist and handed one of the ends to Pedro. "Tie this end around your waist." Woodson spit out water from the waves that slapped painfully against his face. "When we get to the whirlpool's edge, stay far enough away so the rope stays tight." Pedro nodded. "When I give you the signal…" continued Woodson between gasps for breath, "…swim away as hard as you can!" Pedro nodded again.

They fought the raging currents until they swam just short of the still swelling water. Pedro then backed away from the whirlpool until the rope tightened. Woodson threw his end of the rope to Lyons. The professor grabbed for the rope with one hand, but before he could fully grasp it, the rising current quickly pulled him away. Woodson gathered the rope up and, still fighting the currents, somehow managed to throw the rope to Lyons again. This time the professor was able to snatch it with one hand.

"Hold on, Professor!" cried Woodson. "Form a chain and we'll pull you out!"

One by one, they struggled to reach each other, and locking their arms together were finally able to form a chain. Woodson gave Pedro the signal to swim away. They swam against the horribly strong current with all of their might, but it was no use. Even with their combined strength, Woodson and Pedro could not pull Lyons and the others from the whirlpool's mighty grip.

"Look!" screamed Blue, pointing wildly toward the waterspout. "What in the world is that?"

Woodson glanced up; a thick white cloud was forming quickly over the whirlpool. The thicker it became, the lower it descended toward the river's surface. Woodson found something about the shape of the cloud familiar and reassuring. Even in the cold water of the river, a feeling of warmth spread over him. He suddenly felt safe and unafraid. Lower and lower, it dropped until the cloud covered the swirling waters around them. As the lowest wisps of the mysterious white cloud touched the water, the wind began to die, the waterspout retreated beneath the river's surface, and the whirlpool slowly dissipated.

As the currents began to ebb, Woodson and Pedro were able to pull their companions free from the slowing whirlpool. Once free, Woodson and Pedro helped the others swim for shore.

By the time they had all reached the bank, the second boat had already beached. Blue, Keh and the boatman helped the others out of the water when they reached the muddy shore. Soaking wet and exhausted, they sat down in the soft river grass to catch their breath.

Once everyone had stopped gasping, Blue stood up and pointed toward the river.

"Okay, people, can somebody tell me what that was all about?" she asked incredulously. "Did you see that white cloud? I could have sworn it looked like a..."

"...Woman?" said Pedro, finishing her sentence.

CHAPTER ELEVEN
The Question

At last, the afternoon sun had peeked through the heavy gray clouds. Woodson directed Pedro and Hernándo to search the river for any equipment or supplies that might have washed up on shore. Blue and Carla were busy laying things out on the bank to dry while the others set up camp. Woodson stopped to give Panzer a hand with one of the tents.

"Well, now what do we do?" asked Panzer.

"Well Jon, it looks like this expedition is on foot from here on," he replied.

"Wait a minute," snapped Panzer. "According to the map, it could be twenty miles or more until we reach the bend of the river!"

"I know," said Woodson, busy hammering a stake into the ground, "but I don't see any other way."

"Look, I've got an idea," began Panzer, "Hernándo, Lyons, and I will take the boat to the bend. Then, I'll send Hernándo and one of the boatmen back for you and the others."

Woodson leaned against a tent pole and quietly stared out toward the river. He was impressed that everyone was finally working together. All differences appeared to be put aside. He had even seen Hernándo helping Keh with his tent. They were becoming a team and he did not want to split them up.

"Sorry Jon," said Woodson, "we stay together!"

"What?"

"You heard me," replied Woodson. "There's no way that I'm going to split this party up when we don't even know where we are!"

"Look! I'm paying you to—"

"That's right, *Mr. Panzer*, you *are* paying me to do this job. *Now let me do it!*" Without another word, Woodson dropped the tent pole and walked away.

The hot afternoon sun had done its job well. It had dried out nearly everything salvaged and usable. Woodson sat by the edge of the river so involved in translating the pottery shard from the little village that he did not notice Blue and Pedro as they came up behind him.

"There he is, Pedro, working again as always," teased Blue. She squatted next to Woodson and gently placed a hand on his shoulder.

"He never stops," remarked Pedro, bending to see what the archeologist was working on.

"Well, look who's here," he said with smirk. "If you guys would lend a hand now and then, I—" Blue grabbed the brim of Woodson's leather hat and pushed it down over his eyes. "Hey, cut that out!"

Blue pulled his hat back up and knelt down so they were face to face.

"You are missing one beautiful sunset, Richard Woodson!" she exclaimed.

"I know, but I've finally finished this translation." Woodson straightened his hat before holding the small piece of pottery in front of his friends. Blue and Pedro could sense the excitement in his voice. They had heard it before. "This shard looks to be the real deal. It looks and feels exactly like Panzer's map shard. They may have even come from the same piece of pottery. Who knows? Here check this out!"

Pedro took the shard and Woodson's scribbled notes. After a few minutes of study he said, "Woody! They experienced the same thing that Keh did at the little village."

"Can I see it?" asked Blue.

"Go ahead," Woodson replied. "Read it out loud."

Blue stepped back and turned away from the sunset to catch the last glimmer of light from the falling orange sun. Woodson watched as the soft glow from behind made her appear as a featureless silhouette. Blue cleared her throat:

I must warn the people to stay away from the village we call, The Little Place of Evil. Sometime after we arrived, strange and mysterious things began to happen. There are many nawal here. We can feel them. They exist. Some days they allow us to see them. They scare the women and children as they sweep over the village like lost birds in the night.

The men are powerless to stop them. Even our strongest warriors fear their power. I wonder what must have happened in this place for these spirits can find no rest.

I offered a sacrifice to Ix Tab, the goddess of all those fortunate enough to die in battle or sacrifice, with hopes that she will lead these wretched souls to paradise. The nawal come more often now. These souls find no peace. We must leave this evil place.

Our scouts say they have found our new home. The trip will be a treacherous one for the place we are to build our new city. The scouts say the path is very steep with much danger. That is all I know.

We must succeed in building a city that the invaders cannot find. We will build a new city, a city where our people will never need to answer to the kingdom of Tula or its false god, Quetzalcoatl. Our path is clear. We must be allowed to worship Kukulkán!

Today we make for the river. I leave this message on pottery for there is no time to leave it in stone. For the unfortunate one who may find my message, leave this village and come here no more. This evil is more than human beings can bear.

Blue glanced up from Woodson's translated page and inquired, "Who's this Ix (pronounced ish) Tab character anyway? I don't remember her from Mayan History 101."

"May I?" Pedro inquired politely. The young apprentice was grinning from ear to ear. Woodson smiled.

"Ix Tab is kind of like the Mayan goddess of death," Pedro continued, his demeanor suddenly turned very serious as if he were giving a report in class. "My people believe that those who committed suicide, those who died in battle and women who died during childbirth needed help in finding their way to the Underworld. Ix Tab would help them in their travels. I guess you can call her a kind of guide to Mayan paradise."

"Old woman hanging from the sky?" asked Blue, suddenly remembering her college studies. "She wore a noose around the neck?"

"Exactly!" replied Pedro.

"Now I remember Ix Tab," said Blue. "What does it all mean?"

"Not sure," Pedro replied. "You got any ideas, Woody?"

"Nope, I have no idea what happened in that village to stir up the *nawal*. I'm just glad we got out of there when we did."

"What about this line about the path being steep? What do you think that's all about?" Blue asked, pointing to it on the sheet.

"Could mean anything, might be literal, and might not. It's really hard to tell... what *does* puzzle me is the section here about the Toltecs and the relationship between

Quetzalcoatl and Kukulcán. Maybe I should show this to Lyons and Keh. Perhaps they can help."

"I thought that Quetzalcoatl and Kukulkán are one and the same. You know—the great feathered serpent, and all that," said Blue

"I think I can help with that too." Pedro cleared his throat. "You're right; they are the same... in theory. I learned that there was a Kukulcán Cult at Chichén Itzá that defied the Toltec rule. The Toltec brought the worship of Quetzalcoatl with them from central Mexico when they invaded the Yucatan. Even though, publicly the conquered Maya at Chichén Itzá embraced the Toltec sacred god of Tula, the followers of Kukulcán demanded the right to worship in the old ways. The way their ancestors had, as part of a group of gods that ruled every facet of their lives."

Woodson gazed deeply onto the sheet of paper as if he were looking at it for the first time.

"If that's true, then..." Woodson paused.

"Then *what*?" asked Blue.

"... uh nothing, I was just thinking out loud. I'll see you later.

Woodson quickly gathered up the pottery shard and all his notes and headed toward camp. Now there were new facts; facts that he was not at all certain should be shared with his companions.

"Now, what do you suppose *that* was all about?" asked Blue, watching Woodson head back to camp

The sun had set and night was quickly descending on the campsite. Woodson headed directly for Lyons' tent.

"Professor," said Woodson, who did not hesitate to pull the flap back and stick his head inside the tent. "I have something to show—" he stopped just before squeezing through the narrow opening. Lyons and Carla were sitting cozily on the tent floor enjoying a glass of wine.

"Uh... sorry Professor," stammered the terribly embarrassed Woodson. "I didn't mean to disturb you—"

"Quite all right, Woody," replied Lyons, who, Woodson believed to be looking quite happy. "Carla and I were just having a drink. Care to join us?"

"Uh... I think I'd better go... you know... lots of stuff to do. I'll catch up with you later. Goodnight Carla, Professor."

Woodson quickly yanked his head from the tent and pulled the flap down. Carla's giggle and the clinking of wine glasses were all he had to hear before looking for Keh. Woodson was certain he would not find himself in an embarrassing situation at Keh's tent. However, having learned his lesson, he called out before entering.

"Keh? Are you there?" There was no answer. He called out again. This time he heard Keh's voice, but not from within the tent—it came from the center of the camp.

"I am here, my young friend," said Keh. "I am sitting at the fire."

"I have something to show you," said Woodson. He pulled up next to Keh. There was an odd chill in the air this evening and the warmth of fire felt good.

Woodson read the pottery shard translations to Keh. The old shaman made no comment. He just stared into the blazing campfire.

"The fire feels good tonight, my young friend," he said finally. "You are very brave. You did not hesitate when you knew your companions needed your help."

"I did what I had to do," replied Woodson.

"You always do. Do you not?"

"I guess so." Woodson removed his hat and scratched his head. "I never thought about it before, I just do it. If that's bravery... then I guess I'm brave." He pointed at the pottery shard. "What about the people of the village? What do you think happened to them?"

Keh held his hands out to warm them by the crackling fire. Woodson watched as the shaman drew the fire's heat into his old body. Keh had covered his shoulders with a large, heavy blanket. The shaman now looked much older to Woodson. The night was far from warm, but it was certainly not cold, yet the old man appeared chilled from the air and yearned for the fire to warm his spirit.

"What happened to them is not important. I want to know what happened to you and Pedro at Chichén Itzá."

"That's not important," Woodson protested. "I need to know what happened in that village. I am in charge of this expedition and responsible for the safety of everyone!"

Slowly, Keh turned toward Woodson. The old shaman smiled. Keh placed his hand firmly on the younger man's shoulder. "To me, what you experienced at the Sacred Cenote is important, my son." Keh pulled his hand away and once again turned his gaze toward the fire. "I must know about *Guerrero!*"

CHAPTER TWELVE
The Fifth Codex

Woodson sat speechless. Keh stared silently into the fire. One word rang loudly within Woodson's brain. *Guerrero!* A gust of wind suddenly swept through the camp. Woodson covered his eyes as tiny sparks jumped from the fire and danced around his head. Talking about Guerrero and The Fifth Codex had become difficult for Woodson. He understood that there was some kind of spiritual connection between himself and this hero from the distant past. Woodson wanted to reply, but could not. He gazed deeply into the fire.

"My young friend," said Keh, leaning forward in an attempt to make eye contact. "Are you well?" Woodson remained silent.

Blue was out for a walk across the camp when she noticed Woodson and Keh sitting by the fire. Not realizing the situation, she sauntered over and sat next to Woodson.

"Hey Woody," she said playfully, "How about we get something to eat? I'm starved!" Woodson never acknowledged she was there. Blue immediately sensed something was wrong. He never passed up a chance to tease her about her voracious appetite.

"Woody, are you okay?" she inquired, trying to snap him out of whatever was bothering him. "What gives here? Did I interrupt something?"

Woodson pulled his gaze from the fire and looked at Blue.

"Just lost in thought, I'm okay," he said half-smiling.

"Can you tell me about Guerrero?" asked Keh.

"Guerrero!" Blue exclaimed. "Don't bring that up again!"

"I think I'm okay," he replied softly. Then looking back at Keh, "From the beginning?" he asked. The shaman nodded.

"Are you sure you want to do this?" warned Blue. "Talking about it always gives you the creeps."

"Yes. Blue, I'm sure!" Woodson collected his thoughts. He stared into Keh's eyes. "Well, I guess the best place to start would be at the Mayan ruins at Chichén Itzá. About three years ago, Lyons and Pedro found a cylinder containing a journal that was written by Geronimo Agui—"

"Pedro was there?" Keh interrupted. "He would have been quite young, would he not?"

"Yes," replied Woodson. "You see Pedro lived with Angel after his parents had died. Both Angel and Pedro's father were friends with Professor Lyons."

"So of course Pedro accompanied his father's friend to Chichén Itzá," said Keh, speaking more to himself than to Woodson. "Please continue."

Woodson took a deep breath before continuing. "Aguilar was Guerrero's friend and companion, shipwrecked on the Yucatan, along with about a dozen crewmembers. This happened in the early 1500's making them the first Spaniards to set foot in the land of the Maya.

"Almost immediately, they were captured by a tribe of man-eating cannibals. One by one, the natives led them away to some vile ritual. Thanks to Guerrero's cunning and leadership, they escaped their captors only to fall into the hands of your people, the Maya. Much to their surprise, the Maya treated them with great respect and kindness. After a few years, all of the Spaniards, except Aguilar and Guerrero had died either of disease or of loneliness. Guerrero loved the Maya. For the first time in his life, he had found love. He eventually took a wife and had three sons. Aguilar despised his captors for no other reason then that they were different.

He swore he would escape and someday return to seek his revenge.

"By this time, Cortés had arrived in Cozumel and was planning the conquest of the Maya and the Aztecs. Hearing of this, Guerrero saw to Aguilar's release and the Maya gave him safe passage to find his compatriots. A small expedition of Spaniards dispatched to discover the two men's whereabouts found Aguilar.

"Cortés had heard that two white men were living among the savages and wanted them returned. Once found by the Spanish, Aguilar returned to Guerrero and begged him to join Cortés. Guerrero refused. He was happy living with the Maya and did not want to go back to his old life. Aguilar handed Guerrero the strand of green beads that he had planned to buy his freedom with and left. Guerrero knew, from that moment on, that he and Aguilar would be forever enemies."

Woodson reached deep into his pocket, pulled out Guerrero's green beads, and handed them to Keh. The shaman held them out toward the fire to get a better look.

"Those are the beads that Aguilar had been given by the Spanish to buy Guerrero's freedom,"

Keh touched the beads to his forehead.

"These beads are not from my people," he supposed. "These beads were made somewhere…very far away, I think."

"I know. The Spaniards brought them. They thought that the simple minded *savages* would do anything to have them."

"I find it funny that the Spaniards would have thought that. At the time that my people, *the savages*, were mapping the stars and building complex cities, the Spaniards were living like animals in cold drafty castles." Keh smiled and returned the beads to Woodson. "How did you come to have these beads?"

"I'm getting to that." Woodson stood and began to pace. Blue had seen this before; Woodson was getting excited. "When Pedro and Lyons found Aguilar's journal, Lyons struggled to translate it. The professor was able to translate enough to understand that there was a book, or codex, of great power and of untold evil. Aguilar was certain this book would make him immortal. He was obsessed with possessing this book. It drove him to madness. It was no wonder that his journal was difficult to translate. Aguilar had become mad. Lyons decided to give it to someone else, someone who he had recently met, and someone who might have a specific interest in this journal."

"Who was this?" inquired Keh.

"*His* name was also Aguilar. He was the ancestor of Guerrero's Aguilar. This modern day Aguilar somehow figured out what his ancestor was pursuing and became obsessed with the book too. After reading his ancestor's journal, he was sure that Guerrero left a journal as well. He offered to pay Lyons if he would help him find Guerrero's journal. They were sure that it was at Tulum in the Yucatan Peninsula. That was the last place that anyone saw Guerrero or his wife, Zazhal ab alive."

"Ah. There *was* a woman," said Keh, with an approving nod.

"Yes," replied Woodson, not certain why Keh had mentioned it. "Now we fast-forward three years to last spring. Lyons and Pedro again find a journal—this time it *is* Guerrero's. Aguilar was right. Guerrero *had* kept a journal. Guerrero was quite sure that he was the first white man to live among the Maya and decided to chronicle his adventures. The problem was that this time the journal was in Old Spanish and Mayan glyphs. Lyons knew that I was on my way to Tulum. He also knew that I was the only one in the region that could effectively understand the odd mixture of glyphs and Spanish.

"Lyons convinced Pedro that he should pretend to find the journal and hand it over to me. Lyons told him that it would benefit both of our careers. Lyons knew that my curiosity and sense of adventure would overcome my better judgment. He was also certain that I wouldn't report the find until I figured out what it all meant. He knew me better than I thought. I translated the darn thing and led Aguilar and Lyons right to the codex. Guerrero had come to possess it and risked his very life to keep it from the Spanish and *his* Aguilar. Unwittingly, *I* led them to The Fifth Codex, the book of the dead."

"The beads, my young friend," said Keh impatiently, "tell me of the beads."

"You sure are interested in those beads." Woodson held the beads in his hand and stared at them for a few moments. "These beads were in the jar with the journal."

"And the codex, what happened to the book of the dead?"

"To make a long story short... it's sitting at the bottom of forty feet of water in the Sacred Cenote at Chichén Itzá, reclaimed, forever, by God L, the god of the underworld!"

"How did this happen?"

"Aguilar discovered that the only way to become immortal was to speak the words from the codex during a human sacrifice."

"Who was he to sacrifice?" Keh asked.

Blue raised her hand.

"Uh... that would be me," she said sheepishly.

"What happened then?"

"The water from the cenote rose up to the rim of the well in the form of a waterspout," Woodson continued. "It literally took the shape of God L and reached out with its misty fingers snatching the codex from Aguilar's hands."

Keh once again took the beads from Woodson and held them close to his chest. "Something else happened at the cenote," he said softly. "Something that even Angel could not explain."

Woodson pulled a handkerchief from his pocket and wiped away the sweat on his brow. Just thinking of the experience at the cenote gave him the cold sweats.

"You're right," Woodson's voice shook nervously. "When—when Blue and I were hanging by the rope over the water we thought that we were goners." Woodson wiped his brow again then quickly stuffed the handkerchief into his pocket. "Pedro and Lyons were exhausted and the watery mist that engulfed the area made the rocks wet and slippery."

"But you were saved."

"Yes, we were. However, here's the weird thing. According to Pedro, he and Lyons were assisted by an old Mayan woman."

"Again, the woman," Keh commented with great delight. "Did any one else see the woman?' he inquired.

"No," said a voice from the darkness behind them. "It was a woman. I saw her with my own eyes."

"Pedro!" exclaimed Woodson and Blue. They quickly turned to see the young man approach. Keh never took his eyes off the beads.

"I believe you," said Keh. "Come, sit by the fire."

"Can you help us?" Woodson asked Keh.

Keh rubbed his chin thoughtfully, staring at the beads. "But Woody, what is *your* connection with Guerrero?" he asked.

"In his journal, he wrote of a recurring vision. He felt that the vision foretold of his death."

"So?"

"I had the *same vision as Guerrero*. Years ago when I was a very young man; long before I even decided to become an archeologist." Woodson dropped to his knees beside Keh.

"Maybe that is why you came here," said the old shaman. "Something was calling out to you; drawing you to us; even as a boy."

"I've thought of that, many times. Can you help sort this out, Keh?"

"Yes! I think I can."

Some miles away, three dark figures sat around another campfire. Smith sat watching sparks as the wind blew them into the air. One hand held a red clay cup filled with tequila, the other a long thin cigar. He wondered what had caused the wind to pick up so. It was not very common in this part of the country.

"You sure are quiet tonight, Smith," said Franz, reaching for the bottle of tequila. "That scares me. It means you're thinking up your next move."

"This Woodson character might just be smarter than I thought," growled Smith. "I think we'd better pay them a visit tomorrow."

"I thought we were headed for the city. The chicleros should have more goods ready."

"I don't want these people to see us with any artifacts. There would be too many questions. Besides, this Woodson might just stumble on to our little treasure trove." Smith stopped and looked around. "What's that noise?"

"That's Hans snoring," Franz replied laughing. "He's just had too much tequila that is all." Franz leaned over and poked at his large friend. "Wake up, you big herring." Hans woke up with a start and rubbed his eyes.

"That's better," snapped Smith. "Now, listen up. Tomorrow morning we're heading over to Panzer's camp. The note I sent him introduced us as archeologists."

"Why bother?" asked Franz.

"Somehow, we have to convince them that they are headed in the wrong direction."

"There isn't going to be any more shooting, is there?" Hans groaned, rubbing his wounded leg.

"Not yet," replied Smith, before draining his cup of tequila.

"Are you okay, Woody?" asked Blue, knowing the negative effect all of this could have on him.

"You know, I feel better now," he replied. "Maybe it is better to talk about my visions."

"Can you tell me about the first time that you had the vision?" Keh asked. "It would help."

Woodson removed his hat and held it by the brim. He felt nervous and uncomfortable.

"Sure, why not. Maybe this *will* help." Woodson took another deep breath before continuing. "Like I told you, I was much younger, eighteen or nineteen. It was New Year's Eve and all my friends had gone out. I was sick with a cold so I decided to stay home. After watching television for a while, I went to sleep. I hadn't been asleep for very long before I started to dream... at least when I woke up I thought it had been a dream."

"Tell me about the *dream*, my young friend."

"It started with a Spanish Conquistador, in full armor, riding a horse. The horse reared up on its hind legs before galloping down a hill to a sandy beach. Then, the next thing I saw was an old man and what looked like a Maya woman on the water in a dugout canoe—"

Keh interrupted him. "Are you sure that you actually saw the woman?" he asked.

Woodson thought for a moment. "You know, now that you mention it, I'm not so sure I really saw her at all. I know she was there!"

"Maybe you felt her presence?"

"Maybe," replied Woodson with a shrug. "Anyway, the next thing I saw was the dugout catching fire. I could see and feel the man burning just as if it was happening to me. It was horrible!"

"Then what happened?"

"I must have been yelling out in pain. The next thing I knew my dad was in the room trying to wake me."

"Did the vision come again?"

"For years I was haunted by it, but I was finally able to bury it deep in my mind. Until..." His voice trailed off.

"Yes." Keh leaned closer to Woodson.

"Until the first time I was at the ruins in Tulum, when it came rushing back. The vision was as vivid and painful as the first time!"

"This is very good, my son," said Keh. His tone was soft and reassuring. "This will help us reach the spirits and soon you will know your *nawal*."

CHAPTER THIRTEEN
The Path

The sun had yet to rise by the time Woodson had gathered his troops and prepared to break camp. The chill and wind from the previous night had disappeared, replaced by heavy, warm, wet air that descended from a gray morning sky. There was a hint of mist in the air that was cause for concern. Woodson knew that hiking through the jungle would be difficult enough for this group, but these were rainforest conditions and it could become very dangerous.

"Great morning, Woody!" said Lyons cheerfully, as he finished packing his tent.

"Yeah, you bet." Woodson replied sarcastically. He looked up at the gray mist-filled sky. "Can I help you with that?" he asked.

"Sure. At my age, I can use all the help I can get."

"Oh? I don't know, Professor, you seemed to be doing pretty well last night!"

"Last night? Ohhh… you mean *last night!*"

Woodson smiled and nodded. "You and Carla seemed pretty cozy the last time I saw you."

Lyons' darkly tanned face flushed.

"Just two people enjoying a little drink, that's all," he protested halfheartedly. Lyons quickly changed the subject. "What's the plan? Are you sure you know what you're doing by going off on foot?"

"First of all, I sent the boatmen back to get another boat."

"Good. The one that repeats everything he hears really gives me the creeps. How do you know they're going to come back for us?"

"I told them I would double their pay if they did. In addition, Hernándo told them that he would hunt them down if they did not. They will be back! As far as traveling by land, I know that it will be dangerous. But look what happened to us while we were on the water."

"I see what you mean." Lyons had barely finished speaking when he heard a voice yell out from the direction of the river. "Did you hear that, Woody?"

Woodson looked toward the bank. "Yeah, I heard it, too. Let's go check it out." As they started walking toward the shore, Woodson called out for Pedro, Hernándo, and Panzer to meet them by the river.

The misty fog hung like a blanket over the dark water. Lyons could barely make out the large object floating slowly toward the shore. Then suddenly, it broke through the fog.

"There! Look to your right!" Lyons exclaimed.

Woodson could see it now. It was coming ever closer. As it cleared the fog, they heard the call again.

"Hello! Hello!"

"Who's there?" Woodson's voice echoed over the still water.

"Smith, Professor Smith," returned the voice from off shore, "I'm looking for Jon Panzer."

"He's coming," Woodson hollered back. "Come ashore!" Woodson and Lyons were standing at the river's edge as the approaching boat came into full view. One man stood at the bow of a dugout canoe. Woodson could just make out his face. There was no doubt; he had encountered the man in Belize. Quickly, Woodson grabbed Lyons and pulled him aside.

"That's him, Professor. That's Smith."

"I know. I heard him too!"

"No! That's *the* Smith, the one who sent the note to Panzer!"

"Oh, right. What should we do?"

"Not sure. Follow my lead. If he's the Smith that's selling the stolen artifacts, he might just slip up."

Just then, Pedro arrived at the shore with Panzer and Hernándo close behind. Smith's canoe had come ashore and the boatman was helping Smith on to shore.

"Panzer?" asked Smith. He looked everyone over.

Panzer stepped forward. "I'm Jon Panzer. And you are...?"

"Smith, Professor Dennis Smith. I'm glad you got my note."

"Yes. Thank you for your generous offer to assist us but—"

"No problem. I'm never too busy to help fellow archeologists," said Smith with a quick nod of the head. "So, where are you folks heading?"

"We're on an expedition in search of Site Q.," replied Woodson candidly.

Woodson and Smith stood face to face. Smith sensed recognition in Woodson's blue eyes. Just as he suspected, Woodson was the stranger he encountered on that dark street in Belize and the Pullman bus. Smith knew that it made no sense to continue the charade, but this was not the time or the place for a confrontation. The two men stared each other down, their eyes locked like two bitter enemies ready to go to battle. Smith broke the tense silence first.

"You might as well turn back," he said, a sly chuckle escaping. "There *is* no Site Q." Smith removed his short-rimmed black hat and waved it toward the dense jungle to the south. "We've been looking for months and all we've found are some small mounds and buildings of little historical value."

Woodson said nothing, distracted by a second man who stepped from the canoe onto the shore. He was small bearded man. Woodson recognized his face as well. He was definitely one of the sailors he had seen in the cantina in Belize. There was a third man, but this one remained in the boat, the second sailor no doubt.

"Thanks Professor..." responded Woodson. "Did you say your name was, Smith?" Smith nodded. "But I think since we've come this far, we might as well take a look around for ourselves." Woodson started toward the boat. "Your friend in the boat there, Smith, is he okay?" he asked.

"As a matter of fact," he replied quickly, "he fell down one of those mounds and twisted his ankle."

"Looks like he tore his pant leg, too," observed Woodson, inching closer to the boat. "I did a year of pre-med. Want me to take a look?"

"No, thanks," replied Smith casually stepping between Woodson and the boat. "I'm sure he'll be fine. Look, Mr. Panzer, we'd love to stick around and help your expedition, but it's starting to get wet out here and I'm afraid the jungle could get dangerous."

"I think we'll be fine," snapped Woodson. "Thanks anyway."

"Okay, but if I were you, I would stay along the river. If you get too deep into the bush, you may never find your way out."

"Hernándo, here, will get us back," said Panzer. "He knows the area."

Smith looked at the guide and smiled.

"I'm sure he does, Mr. Panzer," he said. Smith turned to the boatman. "Let's move out. I can't wait to get out of this rotten jungle."

Smith and the bearded sailor stepped back in the boat. The boatman pushed it back into the river turning the bow to the north. Smith smiled and waved as they disappeared back into the gray misty light of the dawn.

"All right, everyone," shouted Woodson, once the small boat was well on its way down the river. "I want everything packed up and ready to go ASAP! Pedro, stick around. I need to talk to you."

"He was definitely trying to throw us off the track," said Panzer.

"No doubt, Jon," Woodson said quietly. "But I still think we need to keep an eye on Hernándo. Agreed?"

Panzer nodded and went back to packing up his gear. Woodson grabbed Lyons and Pedro, each by the arm, and pulled them toward the river.

"Don't worry, Woody." Pedro puffed out his chest. "I'll keep an eye on Hernándo."

"We both will, Pedro," said Woodson. He felt a smile tug at the corners of his mouth.

"What do you think we ought to do, Woody?" asked Lyons.

"Actually, Smith *did* give us some good advice. We'd better keep as close to the river as possible. We'll scout the bush, but we need to always know how to get back to the river. Is that understood?"

"How?" inquired Pedro.

"I brought along some whistles," said Woodson, sounding extremely satisfied with himself.

"Whistles?" asked Pedro, the young man's face puckered with doubt.

"Everyone will wear one around his or her neck," replied Woodson. "When a party is away from the river, they must signal every five minutes. Got it? By the way, did either of you guys see the pant leg on the injured man in the boat?"

"Yes, his pants were torn just as you had said," said Lyons. "So?"

"I think I saw some traces of blood further up the leg." Pedro added enthusiastically.

"Exactly, we weren't attacked by banditos the other night!" exclaimed Woodson.

The mist finally started to break up as the sun rose higher into the sky. The river was calm that morning, only the sound of an occasional jungle bird calling to its mate broke the eerie almost touchable silence. Smith sat quietly at the front of the small aluminum canoe. Franz could tell that Smith was deep in thought, and as much as he wanted to speak, he knew better than to bother him. Instead, he turned his attention to his injured friend, Hans.

"How does it feel today?"

"Still hurts real bad," Hans gasped. He gently touched the inflamed wound. "When can we get me to a doctor, Franz? This thing is getting worse!"

"Why didn't you cover that leg up, you big oaf!" growled Smith, turning on his two companions. "Now, Woodson knows that we're the ones that attacked their camp the other night."

"So, what of it? They can't prove a thing!" protested Franz, defending his friend.

"Maybe you're right Franz, it's their word against ours," conceded Smith. "None of that matters if we get caught stealing antiquities from Site Q. and we can't let that happen!

"Then, what should we do?"

"First, we had better get your friend to a doctor. Then you and I are going to head to the site."

"Then what?"

"I'm not sure, Franz, but this lost city is making me *way* too much money to just walk away. I'm going to do whatever it takes to keep this thing a secret and *you're* going to help me!"

Franz could not miss the bluish, spidery veins sticking out on Smith's forehead and neck when he spoke. Slowly, Franz backed away and nodded. He'd dealt with Smith for years and knew that when Smith acted like this, he had better not disagree.

The light mist still rained down steadily on Woodson, Pedro, and the others as they headed south along the river. Three hours had passed since the expedition broke camp. Woodson had taken the lead with Panzer just behind. Blue and Carla followed, with Keh and Lyons bringing up the rear. Pedro and Hernándo had taken the first scouting assignment into the bush. As planned, all could hear the whistles as they sounded every five minutes to keep the separate groups in contact.

Woodson decided that three hours was enough and that everyone could use a break. He signaled for Pedro and Hernándo to return and report

"Did you see anything of interest out there?" he asked upon their return.

Hernándo answered first, "Nothing. Maybe Smith was right. Maybe it doesn't exist."

"It is possible, but where are the artifacts coming from?" Woodson replied. "There has to be something out here! The people who built the city have left us messages all along the way. There has to be more."

"But we're not even sure what we're looking for, Woody" added Pedro.

"There will be a sign, my friends," said Keh, who had overheard the discussion. "I know that it is near," he continued looking up into the gray sky. "The spirits will guide us."

Woodson nodded. "Keh's right! I can feel it too!"

"Excuse me, Woody," Blue interrupted. "I know that you big, strong men want to discuss the spirits and all, but Carla and I need to use the ladies room, if you don't mind." Blue pointed toward the jungle.

"Okay," Woodson replied impatiently. "Don't go too far, and head straight east. Make sure you answer my whistle when you hear it."

"We're not going that far—"

"*Blue!*"

"Okay, Okay!" exclaimed Blue. She and Carla quickly headed for a little privacy from the men. "How about something to eat when we get back, I'm starving."

"*Go already.*" growled Woodson.

As Blue and Carla disappeared into the brush, the men all picked out a comfortable spot to rest. Woodson sat by the riverbank, going over his notes. Lyons and Pedro settled next to him.

"What do you think you're going to see in those scraps of paper that you haven't already?" asked Lyons.

"Yeah Woody," groaned Pedro. "Maybe there isn't anything here at all."

"I'm not sure about that. But, there has to be something that we're missing… some sort of clue—"

A shrill sound filled the air. It was the high-pitched sound of Carla's whistle. Something was wrong. The whistle blew, repeatedly, as if in a panic. Woodson and Pedro sprang to their feet and ran in the direction of the frantic call. The others fell in behind as Woodson tore through the thick brush. Closing in on the sound, he quickly spotted Carla standing in a small clearing with the whistle in her mouth, frantically signaling for help.

"*Help! Help!*" she screamed, seeing Woodson and Pedro explode into the clearing.

"Blue's-in-trouble!" exclaimed Carla gasping desperately for breath between each word. "She fell down a big hole!"

Woodson arrived at the edge of the hole and grabbed Carla's arms.

"What happened?"

"She's down there," cried Carla, pointing repeatedly at the edge of a hole nearly hidden by thick brush. "One second she was right here talking to me and the next, she was... *gone.*"

"Calm down, Carla. We'll find her!" Woodson exclaimed. Before very long the others arrived. "Here, Professor, take care of her. I'm going to find Blue!"

Pedro joined Woodson at the edge; they could hear the faint, muted sound of a whistle coming from below.

"Are you okay?" Woodson hollered over the edge.

There was a short, scary gap of silence before they heard a reply.

"I think so," said Blue. Her voice sounded faint and distant. "Yuk! I'm all covered in *mud!*"

"I'm going to get some rope and come down there to get you." Woodson yelled down the hole. "Don't worry; we'll get you out of that hole."

"It's not a hole, Woody!" she exclaimed.

"What?"

"It's not a hole. It's a path, a really wet and slippery path."

"A path?" inquired Woodson incredulously.

"Yes. If you're really careful, you could probably walk down."

Woodson grabbed a tree branch that hung over the edge. Holding on, he carefully took a few steps down. "She's right.

It is a path. The jungle has grown so dense around it that it just looks like it's a hole."

Pedro stepped up to the edge to get a better look.

"*The path is very steep with much danger*," he said softly.

"What did you say," asked Woodson.

"*The path is very steep with much danger*," he repeated excitedly. "Woody—the shard—the pottery shard we found at the little village. That's what the scouts told the leader when they found the location of the lost city!" Pedro pointed down the path. "This is it!"

Woodson's jaw dropped before widening into a broad grin.

"Sit tight, Blue. We're coming down!"

CHAPTER FOURTEEN
The Rescue

"Pedro! Head back to where we left the gear and tie everything up into three or four manageable bundles. Professor Lyons and Carla will give you a hand," said Woodson. The plan was quickly coming together in his mind. "Panzer, you, and Hernándo need to cut some long walking sticks so we can manage that steep path."

"What are the bundles for?" asked Pedro.

"There's no way to carry all of our gear down that path. What we're going to do is secure a rope down the path. Then, we loop the bundles to the rope."

Pedro scratched his head and said, "I'm not so sure I get this."

"I'm with Pedro. What are you planning to do?" asked Lyons.

Hernándo looked suspiciously over the edge of the hidden path.

"I think I understand what Professor Woodson is planning. Once we get the rope pulled tight, we can attach the bundles of gear. Then they can slide down the rope above the path."

"Exactly!" exclaimed Woodson. "Walking down that steep path is going to be tough enough even with walking sticks. Holding on to the rope will help. There is no way we can carry the gear, but
if we're careful, we can push the bundled gear down the rope as we go along."

"Very clever, Señor Woodson, but what if we don't have enough rope to get to the bottom?" inquired Hernándo, pulling a machete from his belt. His gaze was busy surveying the jungle around him, looking for serviceable branches to act as walking sticks.

"We tie off the end that goes down the path in the best possible area to take the bundles off the rope. Then, we repeat the process until we get to the bottom."

"It could work," admitted Panzer. "I was beginning to have my doubts about you, Woodson, but now I know I picked the right man to lead this expedition."

"Thanks Jon," said Woodson appreciatively

"Uh… Woody," Interrupted Pedro. "How do we get the gear back up the path when we return?"

"I haven't quite worked that out yet."

"Oh great," cried Panzer shaking his head.

Woodson threw up his hands and cried, "Nobody's perfect."

"Hey, what's going on up there?" cried Blue's muffled voice from down the path.

"Are you okay?" Woodson hollered down the path.

"I'm cold, wet, covered in mud, every bone in my body aches, and I'm really, *really* hungry!" her voice sounded shrill and raspy.

"If she's hungry, then she's okay," remarked the smiling Pedro.

"Hold on just a little bit longer!" cried Woodson, trying not to laugh. Taking off his hat Woodson ran his fingers through his neatly trimmed hair. "What do you feel, Keh?" he asked, turning to the old shaman.

The old man moved closer to the edge. Quietly staring at the steep grade before him, Keh placed his hand on the branch of a sprawling tree that grew next to the path.

"This is the sign I spoke of," he said, turning his attention toward the clouded gray sky. Beams of misty sunlight burned through the clouds trying desperately to clear the day. "More important, Professor Woodson, what do *you* feel?"

Woodson stepped back away from the path's slippery edge. He was not exactly sure of what he felt. Having been more interested in figuring out a way down that path, Woodson had not thought about his own feelings. He stepped back to the edge.

"My answer is down there, isn't it?" he asked softly, still peering over the edge.

Keh looked at him and smiled.

"Yes! Down there you will finally find peace," replied the shaman softly.

"What about me?" inquired Pedro.

Keh gazed into the young man's eyes. Pedro felt a shiver crackle down his spine. The old man hesitated before he replied.

"I cannot feel what awaits you down there, Pedro. I am sorry."

Pedro nodded sadly before heading back for the gear.

Woodson looked over the edge and wondered what could possibly be down there. Was this truly the resting place for the elusive Site Q.? Did fate bring him to this remote spot in the jungle? Or was it the spirit of Guerrero?

"All right," said Woodson, snapping out of his reverie. There was a lot of work to do and everyone was waiting for the order. "Everybody knows what they're supposed to do so let's get moving!"

Hernándo and Panzer finished cutting the walking staffs at just about the same time that Pedro stepped into the clearing, dragging the first bundle of equipment. Once they had everything ready for the descent, Woodson began to lay out his plan.

"Listen up! I'll go down first and attach the rope to a tree and—"

"No!" exclaimed Pedro. He snatched up the coil of rope that lay at Woodson's feet. "I'll go down first. We need you up here."

"What do you think you're doing?" protested Woodson.

"We need you up here," replied Pedro. "I'll go down there and tie off the rope!"

Woodson stared at his young friend and said, "My *nawal* is down there, Pedro. Do you remember what you told me on the river?"

"Yes, I am afraid of what might be down there." Pedro glanced at the path's edge that, thanks to Hernándo's machete, was now in plain view. "I need to do this!"

"Okay," sighed Woodson. "Then, wrap that end of the rope around your middle and grab one of the walking sticks that Hernándo cut and get down that path. Comprende?"

"Si," replied Pedro.

"If Angel finds out that I let you—"

"I won't tell him if you don't."

Woodson reached into his pocket and pulled out a chocolate bar.

"Here, I almost forgot, this is for Blue. You *know* how hungry she gets," he said laughing.

Pedro took the bar and stuffed it into his shirt pocket. Then, without another word, he tied the tattered end of the rope around his waist, and took a deep breath before stepping over the edge onto the path below.

It was a good thing for Pedro that he had the rope around his waste. Had it not, his first step well might have been his last. Almost immediately, he slipped on a slick rock and slid down the muddy slope. Woodson pulled the rope tight just in time. Another few feet and Pedro would have slid off the path and over a small cliff. As the shaken young man peered over the edge, he spied the jagged rocks below.

If not for the rope, he would have probably fallen to his death.

"You okay?" cried Woodson. He felt the slack in the rope as Pedro scrambled back up the path to safety.

"I'm okay Woody! I've moved up to better footing now. That first step is pretty tricky, so be careful!"

Pedro checked out his surroundings before looking down the path. It was evident that the years of constant rain and humidity was what had made this path so treacherous. Pedro had been on paths like this before. It was typical for a rain forest. A thick umbrella of trees and vegetation that had probably blocked most the sun's rays since the beginning of time covered the path. Large, slippery rocks jutted out everywhere making the footing even more difficult. The only thing that you could possibly hold on to was an occasional tree root, but they were slippery as well.

Digging the walking staff into the mud with every slippery step, Pedro was able to maintain his balance. The trek down the path was treacherous, but as he began to coordinate the movement of his feet with the staff, he realized that it was not impossible. Pedro had no idea of how long he had been descending the path. Being unsure of how far he needed to go to reach Blue, he called out, hoping to get some idea of how much farther it was.

"Blue! Can you hear me?"

"Pedro, is that you?" he heard her raspy reply. "Where's Woody? I thought *my hero* was coming to save me!"

"He was," chuckled Pedro. "This was my idea."

"Hey! You're sounding pretty close, Pedro. Wave or something, maybe I can see you through the jungle."

Pedro stopped and waved one hand over his head.

"Nope, still can't see you. Are you still waving?"

"Wait! I'll come down a little farther."

Pedro struggled down the path about another fifteen feet. "Can you see me now?"

"No not yet," she replied. Blues heart pounded like a drum.

Pedro struggled down another ten feet. "Can you see me now?"

"No."

"Wait! I think you should be able to see me real soon!" Pedro took one more step. Losing his balance, he fell sliding and bouncing quickly down the path. "Whoa!" he cried, sliding over the rocks and protruding roots. No matter what he did, he could not stop his fall. Faster and faster, he slid down the hill until Woodson pulled hard on his end of the rope causing Pedro to come to a dead stop just at Blue's feet. He looked up at the mud covered Blue standing over him, her hands placed firmly on her hips.

Blue looked down at the mud covered Pedro and smiled. "I think I can see you now, Pedro," she said. They looked into each other's mud covered faces and began laughing.

The steep path had given way to a much more manageable grade. Pedro stood up and attempted to brush the mud from his clothing.

"Give it a rest. This stuff is on for good. I've never seen anything like it!" exclaimed Blue, pointing at the reddish, muddy stains all over her clothes.

"Here! Help me tie off the rope," said Pedro. He untied the knot from around his waist.

Woodson peered over the edge. "Pedro! Are *you* okay?" he called out. Blue answered.

"Don't worry Woody, I saved him. He's tying the rope off now," she hollered. She gave Pedro a hand tying off the rope.

Once Pedro and Blue got their end of the rope tied off, Woodson and Hernándo pulled it tight on their end, tying it off on a sturdy knurled branch that hung low over the path.

Let's see," began Woodson. "It would be best to go down in pairs. Professor, you, and Carla go first. Panzer, you, and Keh follow. Hernándo and I will bring up the rear with the gear. Hold on to the rope with your right hand. Lead with your staff, then the left foot. Once your left foot is set, move the right one down to it. Got it?"

"How do you know how to do this?" inquired Panzer.

"This path is very similar to the one in the rain forest on the island of Grenada, which leads down to the Waterfall of the Seven Sisters. It wasn't quite as steep as this one, but the same technique should do the trick." Woodson vigorously tested the knot that he had just tied. "Blue and I were there about three years ago."

Lyons started to laugh and said, "Oh yeah, I remember. Blue showed us the picture she took of your butt all covered with mud. If I remember correctly, she told me that you spent more time on it than on your fee—"

"That's enough, Professor," replied Woodson, quickly cutting him off. "I think its time to start down the path! Okay?"

Lyons grabbed the rope in his right hand and started down the path. As soon as the professor had gotten about six feet down the path, Woodson helped Carla, who looked extremely apprehensive, up to the edge.

"Don't get too close to the person in front of you," Woodson directed the others sounding as calm and collected as if they were all about to take a simple walk in the park. "If you start to slide, they need time to react so that they can help you."

Carla balked at taking her first step.

"I don't think I can do it, Woody," she cried nervously. "It's too steep."

"Don't be afraid, my dear," said Lyons, who turned to give Carla a reassuring smile. "Nothing to it, Carla, just take it one step at a time."

Carla gave Woodson a nervous glance before looking down the path at Lyons. She took a deep breath and quickly let it out. "Well, here goes nothing!"

Once Carla cleared the edge, Panzer grabbed the rope to begin his descent. Woodson helped Keh up to the edge and handed him the rope. "Are you going to be okay, old timer?" he asked.

The old man gave Woodson a quick wink and a smile before heading down the path. Once Keh had started down, Hernándo and Woodson looped the bundles with all the gear onto the rope. Hernándo carefully pushed the first two bundles of gear down the path following closely after them. When the large Mayan had descended a short distance, Woodson pushed his bundles down the rope.

"Be careful, Professor Woodson," Hernándo called up. "The bundles are bouncing off the path and the hill. I'm finding them very difficult to control." Woodson heard a soft tremor of fear in his voice as he spoke.

"Slow and steady," he replied, struggling with his bundles as well. Woodson glanced down the path to check on Hernándo's situation. At just that very moment, the guide lost his grip on the rope. Hernándo was in free fall sliding uncontrollably down the path toward the same cliff that nearly took Pedro to his death. "Hernándo!" Woodson screamed. "Hold on!"

It was too late. Hernándo had disappeared over the edge, and out of sight. Woodson stumbled down the steep wet path as quickly as his own safety would permit.

"Hernándo," Woodson called out again. Slowly he controlled his own slide down the slimy, muddy path toward the dangerous precipice. Woodson was sure it was too late. Hernándo must have fallen. Then, as he drew closer to the edge, Woodson heard a deep guttural, growling sound. "*Hernándo!*" he exclaimed.

"Aaargh!" gasped the guide who hung precariously from a large tree root jutting out from the cliff's edge.

Woodson scrambled close to the edge.

"Hernándo, are you all right?"

"Hurry," cried Hernándo, still gasping for breath. "My hands are starting to slip!"

Ever so carefully, Woodson peered over the cliff's edge. From there he could see that Hernándo was hanging over the edge, his hands desperately wrapped around the large root just a few feet below the top.

Throwing his arm over the edge, Woodson grasped one of Hernándo's wrists. Reaching down to grab the other, Hernándo's hand slipped from the root. Woodson's reach would never allow him to grab Hernándo's other wrist. Woodson then tried, with all of his might to pull the big man up by grasping the one wrist with both of his hands. It was to no avail, Hernándo was far too heavy. Woodson realized that he would fall as well if he continued to hold on. He was losing his grip on Hernándo's thick wrist. Woodson looked helplessly into the large Mayan's dark pleading eyes. Hernándo knew his fate as he felt Woodsons's grip begin to slip away.

Woodson continued to hold on, refusing to let go. Suddenly, he heard the sliding sound of another body coming toward him. Woodson could not look around to see who it was, but did see another hand reach dangerously over the edge and grab Hernándo's other wrist. It was Keh! Slowly, and without a sound, the old man, using strength that

Woodson would never have believed possible for a man of his age, pulled Hernándo safely back onto the path

As the three men lay there struggling for breath, Woodson stared at Keh in disbelief.

Keh simply smiled.

Hernando lay there also staring at the old man.

"You risked your life to save mine," he said, still gasping for breath. "After the way I have treated you."

"Please, do not think about that Hernándo," replied Keh with a quick wave of his hand. "I did what any man would do, especially for a brother."

"I owe my life to you both." Hernándo glanced nervously over his shoulder at the dangerous precipice that nearly succeeded in taking his life. "Please, forgive me for any pain that I have caused," pleaded Hernándo "My life is yours. I will never forget this day."

CHAPTER FIFTEEN
The Lost City

"Well, it's about time you got your butt down here, Richard Woodson," chided Blue, while munching on the chocolate bar Woodson had sent down with Pedro. "What took so long, anyway?"

"Don't worry about me," he replied sarcastically. "I love risking my life to save you every time you get yourself in trouble!"

"What do you mean every time? I never—"

"Oh yeah," Woodson quickly cut her off. "Who wandered off in Chichén Itzá and nearly wound up at the bottom of the cenote? Hmm! Can you tell me that?"

Blue got up on her toes and right into Woodson's face.

"That wasn't my fault," she snapped. "If it weren't for you, and that silly codex, it never would have happened. So there."

Panzer placed his hands on his hips in sheer exasperation.

"What is going on with these two?" he asked impatiently.

"It is how they show each other affection," answered Pedro chuckling. "Watch."

Woodson grabbed Blue, threw his arms around her, and said softly into her ear, "I was so worried about you. Are you okay?"

I'm fine you big lug," replied Blue, pushing Woodson away. "The only thing hurt is my pride. Are *you* okay? Panzer said that you guys had a close call up there."

"I'm fine and so is Hernándo, thanks to Keh." She threw her arms around Woodson's neck and kissed him hard.

Pedro turned to Panzer, laughing and said, "See, they do this every time."

Panzer shook his head. "I hate to interrupt this touching moment, but if you wouldn't mind—*what do we do now?*"

"From here on," began Woodson, "the grade doesn't look nearly as steep as it was to this point. I guess we should probably load up and see where this thing leads!"

The path weaved endlessly through the dense tree-covered jungle. The path cut through areas of water and red mud so thick, it nearly sucked the boots from their feet. Occasionally, when they waded through streams of rock-strewn rapids, the streaming cool water felt good against their hot feet and legs, but the rocks were slippery and always treacherous.

Unable to see the sun through the cloud filled sky and the natural umbrella of trees, it was impossible to know in which direction the twisting path led. The jungle had overgrown much of the path, but not as much as Woodson thought it should have. Someone had been here and recently. Woodson stopped to pick something up from the ground. Lyons and Pedro made their way up the path to see what he had found.

"Check this out, Professor," he said. "Someone has been here."

"Bare footprints and cigarette butts—chicleros," said Lyons

"Who else could it be? Someone stopped here for a smoke. I don't think the ancient Maya smoked this brand." Woodson held up the muddy cigarette butt. "You might think about having that little pistol of yours handy."

"Way ahead of you," replied Lyons. He patted his jacket pocket.

As they pushed on the path become much straighter and the red mud gave way to a darker, rocky soil. Occasionally

Hernándo needed to machete the overgrown jungle that blocked the path. A little bit of the gray sky that hung drearily over the jungle, was beginning to show through the thinning trees. Less vegetation meant that it was possible that the path could soon open up to a clearing. From the distance came the faint sound of rushing water.

"Can you guys hear that?" he asked.

Pedro moved up next to Woodson and cupped his hand to his ear. "Waterfall!" he exclaimed.

"That's what I thought. It sounds like it is just up ahead. Let's check it out!"

Another fifty feet brought them to the edge of a small river. The water moved by quickly, forming rapids as it approached what must have been falls where the faint roar in the distance emanated. Large rocks dotted the water's surface all across the river, causing the foamy water to splash into tiny explosions of white mist.

Woodson wasted no time in assessing the situation.

"The current is too strong to wade through," he began, "We'll have to cross by stepping on the rocks."

Blue moved up to get a better look commenting, "I don't think so, Woody. It looks dangerous to me. Carla! Come here. What do you think?"

Carla moved up the line and stood next to Blue. Glancing up and down the river, Carla's eyes brightened over a wide grin.

"No problem," she stated with confidence. "I can do this! I used to be a gymnast."

Blue leaned into Carla's ear and spoke through clinched teeth, *"How 'bout us girls sticking together here, Carla?"*

"Aw, c'mon Blue," she replied, while rubbing her hands together. "This will be fun."

"You didn't think that steep path was going to be fun," said Woodson.

"I was just scared of the unknown. This is more my style."

"Oh brother," grumbled Blue.

"Don't worry Blue," said Pedro, "I'll help you get across.'

"Great, but who's going to help you?" she said sarcastically. "Remember falling down the path?"

"Very funny," he replied.

"That's enough!" exclaimed Woodson. "There's only one way across. We're crossing on the rocks!"

"I'll go first, Woody," said Carla enthusiastically.

"Suck up," said Blue under her breath, just loud enough for everyone to hear.

"That's enough Blue," snapped Woodson, "or I'll leave you here. Got it?"

Blue grimaced and with her arms folded tightly across her chest walked to the end of the line still grumbling, "I'm going last!"

"Suit yourself," Woodson growled, before turning to the others. "Anyway, I'm going first to make sure that it's safe."

Woodson carefully stepped onto the closest rock to the shore. Black and wet, it looked as slippery as ice on asphalt. His first step, though as awkward as it appeared, was successful.

"See I told this would work," he cried.

Woodson moved slowly along each slippery rock, each one seemed more slippery than the one before it. Woodson lost his footing more than once, but was able to recover before falling. The water churned beneath him as it slapped powerfully against the rocks, making it even more difficult to keep from slipping and falling into the rushing water below. Woodson had gotten about half way across when, suddenly, the rock beneath his front foot gave way. Woodson, as much as he tried, could not keep his balance long enough to make it to the next rock. With a large splash, he fell into the rushing water, barely able to grab the next rock before being swept away by the foaming rapids.

"That was pretty good, Woody," hollered Blue, once she was sure that Woodson was safe. "The routine was perfect, except for the dismount."

"Ha, ha," he replied, pulling himself up onto the next rock. The water was only deep enough to reach his mid chest. "It's not very deep. Start crossing one at a time. Give each other some distance. Oh, and Blue, if you fall in, believe me when I say... chances are real good that you won't melt."

Woodson continued to make his way along the rocks, until he reached the other side. Then, he started back to the halfway point to guide the others along the slippery rock path. One by one, his companions made their way across the river. Once everyone was safely across, they began what Woodson was sure would be the last leg of the journey.

After crossing the river, the path leveled off. The densely treed jungle was thinning out exposing more of the now partially sunlit sky. Woodson was sure that they were getting very close to whatever it might be—the spirits felt strong within him. The feelings grew stronger with every step. Woodson stopped suddenly, pointing down the path.

"There! Up ahead, there *is s*omething up there. I can see it!

Up ahead, blocking the path stood a wall. It was much higher than any he would have expected to surround a typical Mayan city. It rose for nearly twenty feet above the rocky path. From a distance, the stonework appeared different from the neatly fitted stones, which was the customary way the Maya built their walls. *What was different? Could they find a way around it?*

"Look," cried Woodson with delight, as they finally reached the enormous looking structure. "This wall had been covered with stucco!" Woodson dropped his gear and placed both palms flat against the cool gray stone. "It's not a wall. At least, not a wall that runs around a city." Woodson ran his hands over the tiny tiers of stone. The entire wall was one long wide staircase of some kind. The steps were extremely narrow both ends disappearing into the dense brush on either side of the path. "It's the steps of a building! *A big one!*" he cried.

Woodson continued running his hands over the surface of the great stone structure blocking their way.

"Lyons, Pedro, what do you make of this?"

"Ball court," observed Lyons, "I'm sure of it! Look in both directions. The steps run the length of the building both ways. Does it remind you of anything you've seen before?"

Woodson turned his back to the wall, looked up thoughtfully at the thick umbrella of trees, and laughed.

"What's so funny?" asked Blue. Woodson shook his head and smiled. "What is this place, Woody?" Blue's voice sounded more than a little impatient.

"Chichén Itzá," he replied, shaking his head.

"What are you talking about? We're not in Mexico, you big dope!"

"No! No! I didn't mean *the* Chichén Itzá. The stonework and the steps, Blue. Look over there. Pull the branches away from the wall and you'll see what I mean. You've seen this before."

Blue followed the wall to the edge of the path. Carefully pulling the branches back, she peered into the jungle. Meanwhile, on the other side of the path, Pedro struggled with the dense brush as he attempted to locate the other end.

"Woody, is this Site Q?" Panzer asked enthusiastically.

127

Woodson ignored his question and continued to inspect the ancient steps

"This wall is very similar to the construction of the ball court at Chichén Itzá. I'm sure of it. Look at the construction of the steps. The three small buildings at the summit are the same shape, but smaller. This is incredible!"

"No question about it, Woody," Blue replied while still examining the wall on her side of the path. "If these people were truly the refugees from Chichén Itzá, I think we've found their new home."

"Why would the path end here? Why would they build it here and block it?" asked Panzer.

"I can't answer that until we get to see whatever it is that's behind this wall, Jon," replied Woodson, finally acknowledging Panzer. "Funny, at Chichén Itzá, this side of the ball court was surrounded by a short wall. I wonder why they didn't build one here."

"Woody," said Pedro, who was so deep in the brush that no one could even see him. "I bet they figured that the environment was protection enough on this side. I mean, look at this mess!" Woodson's apprentice stuck his head out from behind a large group of bushes. "If I'm right, the shortest distance to the end of the wall should be in this direction. I don't think I can move any farther along. The jungle is too thick beyond this point."

Panzer jumped up onto the bottom step and said, "Why don't we just walk up the steps?"

"Stop!" yelled Woodson. He grabbed Panzer by the arm and led him away from the wall. "Those steps are a thousand years old! There's no telling whether they will hold your weight."

"That's ridiculous! That step looks as solid as a rock!" Panzer exclaimed.

Blue bent over the steps, and with just one hand, pulled a stone from the step that Panzer had just stood on. "That could happen halfway up. Still want to try it?" Blue dropped the stone at Panzer's feet.

Panzer smiled and shrugged. "You win. The jungle it is."

Woodson pointed at the machete that hung loosely from Hernándo's belt.

"Is that thing sharp enough to cut through that brush?"

"We shall soon see, Professor Woodson," replied the large Mayan. Hernándo pulled the large machete from its leather sheath and began to hack his way into the thick, jungle brush. Woodson was certain that this was the last obstacle to keep them from their final destination. If this was indeed, Site Q, it was now within reach.

Hernándo feverishly hacked his way through the dense wet growth, his machete more than equal to the task. The group fell in behind him in single file. Woodson and Pedro cleared the path of the fallen branches that fell behind their guide. Lyons brought up the rear, pistol in hand!

Hernándo continued to attack the stringy vines and prickly brush that blocked their way. Woodson placed his hand on Hernándo's shoulder signaling the big man to stop.

"Stop, "he whispered, hoping that only his companions would be able to hear. "I think we're being watched!"

Though the wall was high, the younger of the two men at the top, was certain they had been spotted. *Why else would they stop?* He thought. The silence was deafening, it felt as if the world was standing still.

"What are they doing?" the young man asked. "How could they have seen us?"

The older man smiled, quietly replying, "They did not see us, my son."

"Then, why did they stop? Could they have heard us?"

"We made no noise."

"Then, what are they doing? Why did they stop?"

"I do not know. We must get word to Smith that they have arrived."

The two men prepared to climb down the ruins. The old man took one last look at the jungle below. *How did you know we were here?*

Keh finally broke the deafening silence. "Did you hear something, Woody?" he asked.

"Not exactly, Keh. It's more like I felt something."

"I felt it as well, one or two?"

"Two I think."

Keh closed his eyes. "As did I."

"Okay, you guys," snapped Blue. "What gives?"

"I'm sure that there were two men watching us from the top of the wall," replied Woodson, still gazing upward.

"They couldn't possibly see us through this dense jungle, could they?"

"Not sure. But, I know they were there." Woodson turned back to Hernándo and tapped the guide's shoulder, "Let's get going. The sooner we get out of this brush, the better I'll like it."

CHAPTER SIXTEEN
More Mystery

The sound of Hernándo's machete, tearing through the thick green branches, echoed against the massive stone wall. Every slash brought them closer to the end of this massive structure blocking their way. The thick jungle suddenly faded away to low-lying brush only about a foot or two in height. They had broken through. There, as the jungle began to dissipate, was the squared off corner that turned at a right angle to the massive steps. There was nothing in their way now.

They found a short rocky path that led to a long, narrow enclosure. It was rectangular, similar in shape to a football stadium. There was no mistake; it was a Mayan ball court. High walls surrounded the thick, brush-covered playing field where the spectators could watch the uniquely Mesoamerican game played below. On each end of the court, there were buildings that no doubt served as temples, but the building that stood directly across from them was the most impressive.

Woodson removed his hat and wiped his brow. He was in awe. The others all gathered around him. There they stood, looking across this ancient ball court at something very familiar. With its square shape and incredibly decorative roof, the small building that stood proudly atop the thick wall overlooking the ball court, appeared to be a facsimile of the Upper Temple of the Jaguars. Five long steps that ran nearly the entire width of the temple led to the ceremonial structure. Two ornately carved pillars framed the small rectangular entryway. Panels featuring, Kukulcán, the feathered serpent adorned the buildings upper facade.

"I don't believe it!" he said. "It is exactly like the one at Chichén Itzá!"

"Not exactly," said Professor Lyons. "Look at the dimensions. It's much, much smaller"

"You're right, it is smaller, but still quite a faithful replica."

Carla walked out onto the court and pointed at the two rings that jutted out from the walls. The rings were directly across from each other and over fifteen feet above the court.

"What are those?" she asked.

"Those are the goals," replied Pedro.

"How?" she asked

"The players would have to hit a small rubber ball through the holes."

"It looks like it would be pretty tough to me."

"It was, considering that the players couldn't use their hands. They wore leather pads around the hips and would hit the ball with them."

"Through that tiny little hole?" asked Carla. She gazed up at the small stone ring. "It can't be more than a foot in diameter!"

"I understand they were quite good at it," said Lyons, placing his arm around Carla's shoulder. He was pointing in the direction of the stele across the court. This dark weathered stone carried the gruesome depiction of what happened to the losers.

"They cut off their heads?" she gasped.

"Maybe," Lyons replied with a sly grin. "That *is* the popular opinion. Personally, I think it was the winners who lost their heads."

"The *winners*?"

"The ancient Maya believed it was an honor to be sacrificed to their gods, so why not the winners?"

"How did such an awful game come about, Professor?"

Lyons rubbed the gray stubble on his chin while collecting his thoughts.

"Let me see. How do I explain this without going into too much detail?" He paused for another moment. "The Maya believed that their ball courts were portals to the underworld, Xibalba. At Chichén Itzá, they celebrated the sons of the Maize God, the mythical Hero Twins. The twins disturbed the Lords of Death while playing their game of ball. Every night, the Lords would attempt to kill them, but all of their efforts would fail. Every day, the twins would challenge the Xibalbans to a game of ball, each always ending in a tie. This angered the Xilbaban gods. The twins knew their death had become unavoidable. Knowing this, they planned a way of dying so they could someday come back to life. Before they died, the twins convinced the gods to throw their lifeless bodies into a fire. Their burnt bones then ground to dust and thrown into a river. The river brought them back to life. Five days later, they returned to the world as human beings. They challenged and defeated the Lords of Death, banishing them to the Underworld, forcing them to leave the human world forever. From this legend came the ballgame that was practiced for nearly a thousand years."

Pedro stared out toward the plaza.

"Where is the Temple?" he asked, "If this is a replica of the ball court, where is El Castillo?" El Castillo, a step pyramid, was the largest structure in the ancient city of Chichén Itzá.

"Maybe we had better take a look around," said Woodson, surveying the plaza that extended out beyond the ball court. "Hernando, let's make camp under those trees over there. If you ladies would be so kind to give him a hand, I'm sure he would appreciate it. Pedro, you and Keh come with me. Professor, I want you and Panzer to head in the direction of what would be the Sacred Cenote. Take a whistle with you. I want to hear it every five minutes—got it?"

"This *is* strange," Woodson commented, as they made for the spot where the great pyramid should have been. "Why duplicate the ball court, but not anything else?"

Woodson gazed suspiciously around the deserted ruins. He spied two smaller pyramids nearly swallowed up by the jungle, where the Temple of Warriors should have been. They now appeared to be little more than large mounds.

"No question about it, Pedro, just the ball court resembles Chichén Itzá. Let's see what else we can find!"

"It is, without question, that these people were either from the Yucatan or, at least knew of it. Why stop at just the ball court? Why not finish the *shrine?*" observed Pedro, as they made their way through the tall, jungle grass.

"You think this is a shrine?"

"The spirit of my people runs very deep; why not build a shrine to the home they once loved? They could not stand to live under Toltec rule, so they came here. Why not make this place look more like their home?"

"That's very perceptive." Woodson turned to Keh. "What do you feel?"

Keh squatted down onto the tall grass taking a deep breath while looking skyward to the gods. "This *is* the place you seek, my young friend. But not for the reason you believe," he said calmly, "but soon, you will know why we are here."

"What do you mean—?"

A shrill, high-pitched sound shattered the quiet air. Lyons was blowing his whistle like crazy. He and Panzer burst from a group of trees. "Woody! Woody!" he shouted. "You are not going to believe this."

Woodson and Pedro started toward them. Keh stayed back, seemingly uninterested in the interruption.

"What is it?"

"Paths, Woody! They're everywhere!" Lyons exclaimed.

"Paths, what kind of paths?"

"There has been all kinds of activity over that way," said Panzer gasping for breath. He pointing toward the trees they just came from. "Broken-up slabs of limestone are everywhere."

"This is it!" exclaimed Lyons. This is where the stelae are coming from. We found what looked like an abandoned campsite. Chicleros—I swear the coals from their fire were still warm!"

"I knew it! I could feel them here," cried Woodson.

Lyons cocked his head and gave Woodson a funny look.

"You know, Woody," he said. "You're starting to scare me."

"You know, Professor, sometimes I scare myself… Keh, get Hernándo, and the girls, I think we'd all better stay together until we know if we're alone here or not."

"There are no others," Keh said softly. "You four go ahead and do what you must. You will be safe. I will stay here and help the others with the camp."

"Are you sure there is no one else here but us?" asked Woodson.

"You are *not?*" the old man replied.

Woodson paused; his face drew suddenly blank and sullen.

"Woody," said Pedro, the first to notice the odd look on Woodson's face. "What's wrong?"

Woodson quickly snapped out of it and replied, "Keh is right. There is nobody here but us… *for now!* Let's go see what damage these people have done to this site before it gets dark."

Just as Lyons had said, they encountered paths running off in many different directions. Entering a small cluster of trees, they followed a path that led in exactly the direction of where the Sacred Cenote would have been at Chichén Itzá. Woodson stopped dead in his tracks.

"Is this the way?" he asked, pulling a small, round compass from his small leather backpack. Lyons glanced at Panzer and both men nodded in agreement. Woodson looked back at the compass. "This path is approximately thirty degrees to the west of due north."

"That would give it about the same relationship as the Sacred Causeway is to the ball court at Chichén, Woody!" exclaimed Pedro. "This is really getting strange."

Woodson beamed with pride at his young apprentice. Pedro had learned much of the ancient Mayan customs and cities. Even though he was only sixteen, Pedro really knew his stuff.

"Let's see what you found, Professor," said Woodson. Pedro led the way down the path, the others bunched together behind him. The brush on the path appeared trodden down, repeatedly and recently, there was no sign of new growth. Someone had been on this path today, Pedro was sure of it. He directed Woodson's attention to the left of the path, where there was a low-lying stone wall, four, maybe five feet in height that reached out for the path from the jungle. Woodson knelt down on the path and pawed at the flattened brush.

Without looking up Woodson held out his right hand like a surgeon waiting for an instrument.

"Pedro, let me borrow your knife." Without looking, he took the knife that Pedro very quickly opened and placed in Woodson's waiting hand. It was obvious to Lyons and

Panzer that they had done this before. Taking the knife in his right hand, Woodson cut deeply into the vegetation. It was only seconds before the knife hit something very hard. It was a rock. He continued to dig. First to the left, then to the right of the first rock he found. More rocks! Everywhere he was able to get the knife through the dense, matted-down brush he found rocks at least as large as his fist. Limestone rocks fitted tightly together as finely honed puzzle pieces.

"*Sacbé!*" he exclaimed. "There's no doubt about it. This is definitely a Mayan road. This *was* their Sacred Causeway!"

"There aren't any sinkholes in Guatemala," remarked Lyons. "All we found were the remnants of broken up stelae! Why build a causeway to a cenote that doesn't even exist."

"Maybe what you found acted as their Sacred Cenote. Who knows what we're dealing with here?"

Again, they set out down the path. Footing became difficult at times because the stones beneath the brush had become uneven from centuries of weathering. Walking down this *sacbé,* or sacred road, brought back memories for Woodson. Memories of Chichén Itzá and the last time he had been on the Sacred Causeway there. He remembered the pain from the bullet that passed through his shoulder when one of Aguilar's goons shot him. How he, Pedro, and Lyons were able to save Blue from drowning in the cenote where Aguilar had attempted her sacrifice to release the evil that dwelt deep within The Fifth Codex. How the spirit of God L rose from the cenote in the form of a waterspout and reclaimed the evil book for the Underworld. And the mysterious Mayan woman, who Pedro said helped pull him and Blue from the depths of the cenote.

The visions he knew he could never forget. It was because of them that he even came to this strange place. The vision that Woodson had thought was a nightmare, so many years ago, turned out to be the underlying force of everything that had happened to him since.

Woodson sensed that his sudden silence had disturbed the others. He did not want them to lose confidence—not now.

"How much farther, Professor?" he asked.

"Just up ahead, Woody. Wait until you see it, a circle of stelae where the cenote would have been in relation to the plaza at Chichén Itzá! Look straight ahead!"

Woodson stopped again. To the best of his knowledge of Mesoamerica, nothing like what he saw existed. There before him, where the Sacred Cenote *should* have been, stood a large circle of limestone stelae, large, dark stone slabs, exactly like the one that he had translated in Panzer's office. There must have been forty or fifty of them. They all faced into the circle. Most of them were complete, but many had had the faces neatly sawed off. In the center of the circle was a large platform with steps that led to a Chac Mool.

Statues of Chac Mool always took its rightful place on Mayan sacrificial platforms. In typical Mayan fashion, a Chac Mool was a reclining figure of Chac, the sacred god of rain and agriculture. Lying upon its rounded back, the Chac Mool's head was up and turned so it could view the gruesome ceremony. Resting comfortably on the statues stomach was the sacred plate where the sacrificial victim's still beating heart was placed as an offering to the gods.

There was no doubt that they had found what they were looking for—where the mysterious stele and other artifacts had come from. Nevertheless, was it truly *Site Q?*

CHAPTER SEVENTEEN
The Vision

The young man tossed and turned trying to find comfort in his sleeping bag. He had awoken suddenly. *Was it a dream*; he thought. He realized that he had fallen asleep with the tent flap open. The pale blue light from the full moon streamed in through the opening, filling the tent with an eerie brightness. He knew it would be impossible to fall back to sleep.

Was it another vision, he thought. He sat up and rubbed his eyes. The images that disturbed his sleep and awoke him so suddenly, were still running through his mind, keeping him awake, making him think.

Standing, he grabbed his hat and stepped out into the night air. It was still warm, very warm, this night in the jungle. He looked up at the full moon. He could not remember ever looking up at another that shone as brightly as the one tonight. Walking over to the center of the camp, he noticed some smoke rising from the nearly extinguished coals of last night's campfire. The young man picked up a long stick and poked the smoldering embers back to life. He was not cold. He did not need the warmth of the fire. It was just something to keep his thoughts company. He knew it was more than a dream. It had to be another vision. He hoped that it was not, there were enough visions haunting him already. He threw another piece of wood on the fire and waited for the sun. Only then would he find the answers.

The small dugout boat pitched downward. As the boatman reversed his oar in the river, the two men sleeping in the back of the boat came to life.

"What in the world are you doing up there?" growled one of them.

"There! Señor Smith! Look!" exclaimed the boatman, pointing toward the shore. There were two men, waving their hands wildly over-head to get the attention of the boatman.

"Who are they?" asked Franz. He shaded his eyes from the morning sun. "They sure seem to be excited about something!"

"Chicleros," snarled Dennis Smith. "I *told those two* to stay put!"

"These men work for you?"

"They do now, Franz. Boatman, pull over to the shore, pronto!"

Slowly, the small dugout turned toward the shore.

"They found it, Señor Smith!" exclaimed the older chiclero, as the boat drew closer to the shore. "They are in the city!"

"What is he talking about, Smith?" inquired Franz.

Smith knew exactly what the chiclero meant. "*Woodson!*" he exclaimed, his teeth and fists clenched tightly.

"How could they have found it?" cried Franz. "You said that the only way into the site was behind the waterfall!"

The older chicleros grabbed the bow of the dugout as it hit the shore. "They did not come that way, Señor. They came up that small path behind the ballcourt. We saw them!" he exclaimed.

"What were *you* doing back there?" snapped Smith.

"My son and I were hungry. We looked in the jungle for plantains," replied the older man, looking down to avoid Smith's glare.

"Did they see you?"

"No."

"Good!"

"Señor?" the younger man stepped forward and politely addressed Smith.

"What?"

"They knew we were there, Señor. I'm sure of it!"

"How could they if they did not see you. Did you make any noise?"

The older man interrupted, "We made not a sound, and it was impossible for them to have seen us, but…"

"But what?" growled Smith, leaning into the older man's face.

"But, my son is right. Somehow," he paused and slowly shook his head, "somehow they knew we were there."

"Get in the boat, you two," Smith said coldly.

"What do we do now?" asked Franz. He helped the two chicleros into the boat.

"We finally put an end to this! Boatman, let's get this boat downriver."

The pre-dawn mist began to break as the morning sun rose above the jungle trees. Woodson remained by the fire while his companions slept. Keh sat beside him. The old shaman had been there since before the dawn. Woodson knew why he was there, but he did not speak. He did not have to.

"You did not sleep, my young friend?" asked the old man. Keh stirred what was left of the glowing coals.

Woodson kept looking into the fire as he spoke, "You need to ask?"

"I did not sleep either, my young friend. You had another vision. I can feel it!"

"Yes."

"Tell me about the woman; Guerrero's woman."

"I don't understand, Keh. What does she have to do with...?" Woodson paused. A look of sheer disbelief crossed his face. "Oh, no, you're right!"

"What was her name?"

"Zazhal ab."

"It means 'the dawn,' does it not?"

"Yes, but I—"

Keh persisted, "Tell me about her Professor Woodson. Tell me all that you know."

"She was the High Priest's daughter, at the city of Dzibilchaltún, in the northern Yucatan. She was very learned in Maya texts and taught Guerrero how to speak and read the ancient language. After a while, she and Guerrero fell in love and were married."

"The codex that you discovered, did she know what that book was capable of?"

"I believe she did. I remember reading from Guerrero's journal that the words and images scared her so that she stopped reading the book to their sons during the escape from Aguilar."

"Now, do you wonder about the woman in your vision?"

"How could you know?"

"Tell me of your vision."

Woodson gathered himself, stood up, and glanced around the camp. It appeared as if no one would disturb he and Keh.

"I was flying over the Yucatan. I wasn't sure, at first, but then I saw the coast and then I saw Cozumel."

"Angel's island?"

Woodson could not help but smile at the old man. He had not really thought about Angel since he met Keh.

"Yes, Angel's island," he said with a sigh. "Then, rising from the center of the island was this large figure of a woman. She was wearing a black hooded—"

"Cloak?" asked the old man.

"Yes... that's right, and then she—"

"Turned into a large black bird and flew—"

"Southwest," cried Woodson before falling to his knees next to Keh. "How could you know all this without my telling you?" He held out his hands as if pleading for the answer.

"I, too, had this vision," replied the old shaman.

"When?"

"Some months ago, I cannot say exactly."

Woodson stood and paced back and forth in front of the fire. He mumbled something under his breath before stopping to glare at the old man.

"Now, I understand everything!" he exclaimed. "Why you've kept asking me about a woman. Why the water-spout appeared in the shape of a woman." Woodson removed his hat and ran his hands through his hair. "Keh, *I know why I'm here!*"

CHAPTER EIGHTEEN
Answers

My father's vision of a new home for his people is now very real. We live in safety and we prosper. The people miss the old city and even more, the old ways. We have created this sacred place for our ceremonies. It is not the cenote but it does serve its purpose. The Portal is nearly finished. Soon we will again play the ancient game of the Hero Twins. This pleases the people.

This place is so different from our homeland. The building stone is not as plentiful as we are accustomed. Because of this, we have abandoned the idea of building another pyramid temple to the god Kukulcán. Instead, we have erected two small mound pyramids for the High Priests to teach the old ways.

Water is plentiful in this place. Sweet, cool water runs along the edge of the city before it falls off the edge of the world. We have learned how to move this water to the fields. The maize grows well here; all crops do. The people are happy and safe, and my father's spirit rests in peace.

"Woody!" Woodson turned in the direction of the voice. It was Blue and Carla. *"Woody!"* Blue called out again.

"Yes, Blue. *What is it?"* he asked impatiently.

Blue and Carla were rushing toward him. Blue was waving a sheet of paper in the air as they approached.

"I've got a question about the translation of the first stele at the circle!" she exclaimed.

"Look ladies, Keh and I are kind of busy here... Would you mind—?"

"*Richard Woodson!*" Blue exclaimed. Her voice sounded more than a little impatient. "*This will only take a second!*"

Woodson shot a glance at Keh, smiled, and shrugged his shoulders and turned back to Blue and Carla.

"That's better." Blue's tone softened. "What I want to know is what does this line about the water falling over *the edge of the world* mean?"

He took the page from her hand and read the translation again.

"I don't know, Blue," he replied impatiently, "these were ancient people far from home. It could mean anything."

"Remember when we crossed that small river? Didn't you say that you thought that you heard a waterfall?" asked Carla.

"What?"

"You don't remember that?" Carla persisted.

Woodson scratched at the week-old whiskers on his square jaw. He realized that he had been so involved in their discoveries that he had forgotten to shave.

"Yes, now that you mention it. Why?"

"We want to go find it," said Blue. "What do you think?"

"Not right now—!"

"Oh come on, Woody! We girls want to have some fun, too. Maybe we'll find it and take a swim. I know *I* could use a bath! I don't know how you guys can stand being dirty all the time! Who knows, I might find more interesting artifacts." Blue waved a threatening finger at Woodson. "I am an archeologist and perfectly capable of finding my way around one of these sites!" Blue folded her arms across her chest, huffed, and tapped her foot impatiently. Woodson glanced down at the tapping foot. He knew the signs. It was no use fighting.

Woodson held up his hands indicating complete surrender and replied, "Okay, okay. Just be careful and don't forget to take your whistles. Ask Lyons if you can take his gun. I would feel a lot better if you took some protection."

"Gun? I haven't shot a gun in years!"

Carla ran a hand through her curled blond hair pulling it off her forehead.

"I have!" she said with a broad smile.

"What?" Woodson wondered why a young, attractive woman like Carla would need to know how to use a gun.

"Downtown Chicago can be a dangerous place for a woman living alone," she replied.

"Okay, then. Tell Lyons that I want you guys to take the gun."

"Yes sir," said Blue. She flashed a quick military salute before she and Carla headed back to their tent.

Keh placed his hand on Woodson's shoulder. "She is very important to you, is she not?"

Woodson smiled as he watched Blue walk away. "Blue?" Woodson turned his attention back to the old man. "Yes, Keh, she is *very* important to me!"

"Are you going to tell your friends?" asked the old man.

"That I know why I'm here?"

"Yes, of course."

Woodson removed his hat and ran his hands through his hair replying, "Not yet, Keh."

"There's something else, isn't there, Professor? There's something that even I can't sense."

"I don't want the others to know this, but I'm not so sure that this place really is Site Q!"

146

"Are you sure you know how to use that thing?" inquired Blue, pointing toward the gun that was now stuck uncomfortably in Carla Jamison's belt.

"No," she replied softly.

"You mean, you *don't* know how!"

"Haven't fired one of these things in my whole life, Blue!" she said proudly.

"Then, why did you tell Woody that you knew—?"

"You wanted to go look for the waterfall didn't you?"

Both Blue and Carla laughed out loud.

"Well, it didn't take you very long to figure Woody out, did it?" chuckled Blue.

Carla placed her hands on her hips and batted her eyes.

"He's a man, isn't he," she replied, still laughing.

They started down the narrow path that led from the stelae circle into the jungle. The trees were dense, but the chicleros had traveled the small path recently. The cigarette butts and paper litter along the way made it easy to follow.

"The chicleros, that are raiding this site, sure aren't the neatest folks. What a mess they've left," stated Carla, as they entered a dark thicket of trees.

"It's pretty standard for looters. Not much respect for the ancients. Raiding these ruins is a way of life for these people. It's hard to worry about a bunch of old rocks when your children are starving," explained Blue. The trees above them grew thicker, thick enough to block the sun.

"It's too bad that there can't be some type of compromise. You know, governments, archeologists and locals all working together."

"That would be nice, Carla. The local governments throughout Central America are so corrupt and the people so poor, that it would be impossible. Anyway, even if you could bring them all together, there would still always be somebody like this guy Smith around to ruin it."

147

"Wow, Blue, it's getting really dark. The jungle is getting thicker and thicker."

Blue grabbed Carla by the arm.

"Shush," she hissed, glancing first to her left, and then the right. She then looked up, and then down the path.

"What is it, Blue? Did you hear something?" Carla asked.

Blue detected a little bit of fear in Carla's voice.

"Lions and tigers and bears, oh my!" she said giggling.

"Blue!"

"Sorry, I couldn't resist. Look there's a clearing up ahead. Let's see what's up there."

Blue led the way down the path, Carla right on her heels, hand resting on the handle of the gun. As they drew closer, they could distinctly hear the sound of rushing water. In the clearing, they found what must have been the same river that they had waded through the day before. This time, the noise was different. The sound of water roared as it crashed hard upon the rocks below.

"The falls must be close. Can you hear it?" cried Blue, grabbing Carla's arm pulling her toward the sound. Within a few hundred feet, they came to the edge of a cliff. Looking down, they watched the water rush over the edge and crash onto the rocks below. The cascading water formed a large, blue pool. The pool looked extremely calm and inviting, but from where Blue and Carla stood, it appeared that reaching this prize would be quite impossible.

Blue quickly noticed that the path did not end at the edge. It descended the base of the cliff at a pitch just steep enough to allow them to proceed safely.

"Let's follow the path. Maybe it goes down there," said Blue, pointing toward the picturesque blue water below. "I sure could use a bath."

Carla leaned over the edge smiled and said, "Me too."

Woodson, Pedro and the others entered the sacred circle of stelae. Armed with plenty of tracing paper and pencils, they began the work of copying the fragile history of this strange city and the people who had built it.

"What do you make of all this?" asked Lyons, as he spread a large sheet of white tracing paper over the face of a gray limestone stele.

"I'm really not sure, Professor, but I *am* sure of one thing; the architecture here is more Puuc then Toltec, with absolutely no Quiché, or Guatemalan Maya influence at all. These people were definitely from the Yucatan!"

Panzer and Hernándo were busy clearing jungle that covered most of the stelae in the circle. Pedro and Keh stood by the altar located at the center, locked in a heated debate about how the Maya of this strange city might have performed their ritual sacrifices.

"Could this be Site Q?" asked Lyons without looking up from tracing the stele.

"Bear with me, Professor," began Woodson. "First of all, these people were like pilgrims looking for religious freedom."

"Yes, the Cult of Kukulcán. I understand."

"They more than likely hated the Toltec invaders, so they came here. I agree, it's a long way from home, but I think they were desperate." Woodson started to pace back and forth. Lyons knew he was in for one of Woodson's long speeches, so he decided to make himself comfortable on the stele he had been tracing. "So, they came here and built a monument to the way of life they loved. The style is very Puuc. The way Chichén Itzá was before the Toltec invaded. Look at the ball court. Yes, it's laid out exactly like the one at Chichén Itzá, but... different. You saw it!"

"Look Woody, I—"

"Hold on! I'm getting to my point." Woodson knelt down in front of Lyons and pulled out a small notebook. "Because they were so isolated here, there was no Quiché Maya influence from neighboring cities. Here look at my notes,"

Lyons quickly scanned the top page of the notebook Woodson handed him.

"I see where you're going with this," he replied.

"I thought you might. I was pretty sure that you were thinking the very same thing I was."

"That many of the artifacts from *Site Q.* have been of Quiché Maya?" Lyons responded with a question.

"Which means that if this is Site Q., why is there nothing but Puuc influence, including all the artifacts we have found? If Site Q. is, indeed, in Guatemala and there have been Quiché stelae found on the black market that have supposedly come from there, then why is there no trace of it here?" Woodson shook his head. "I'm afraid that this isn't Site Q."

"Are you going to tell Panzer? He thinks he's died and gone to heaven."

"I know. He thinks that this is Site Q. and I'm not so sure that there is such a place."

Pedro suddenly appeared from behind.

"Well this sure isn't, Woody," he snapped.

Startled, Woodson jumped to his feet. "Pedro!" he exclaimed. "I didn't see you there."

"Look, there's something funny about this place." Pedro rubbed his upper arms as if he felt a chill. "I'm really sure that this isn't Site Q."

Woodson brought a pointed finger to his lips, "We've already figured that out. Shhh! Panzer might hear you."

"Somebody's got to tell him, this place is a mistake or something."

"We know," said Lyons speaking softly. "There is no Guatemalan influence here at all."

"The glyphs are all Yucatan," began Woodson, "but the stele I saw in Panzer's office was too." Woodson pointed toward the circle of limestone slabs that dotted the area. "None of this stuff matches what we believe to be from Site Q."

Lyons ran his hand slowly across the limestone stele.

"Smith must have just recently come upon this place," he said. "He probably stumbled onto it by accident—"

Pedro quickly interrupted the Professor, "And smuggled some of the stelae out of the country saying it was from Site Q. Panzer got his hands on one and became obsessed with finding Site Q."

"Exactly!"

"And we just happened to be the people that he chose to find it." Woodson fell silent, his eyes glazed over.

"What's wrong?" asked Pedro. "Are you okay?"

"The spirits!" he replied excitedly.

"What spirits?" asked Lyons.

"The spirits, Pedro, I know that you felt them too!"

Pedro closed his eyes and nodded.

Woodson glanced at Keh who still stood by the altar admiring the Chac Mool. The shaman turned—instantly their eyes met. A wide grin split the old man's face. *He knew!*

"Look, Carla. There's a cave!" Blue exclaimed, noticing that the path had ended in shadows of black.

As they reached the opening, the sound of crashing water rattled off the dark cave walls. They could feel the vibration of the water as it crashed over the rocks and into the waiting pool below.

We are *really* close!" exclaimed Blue, barely able to hide her excitement. "I can almost feel that cool water all over—"

"Do you think we should go in there? It looks dangerous," interrupted Carla, knowing what Blue's answer would be.

"I bet it's the only way down to the falls. C'mon Carla, where's your sense of adventure?"

"But it's really dark in there!"

Blue pulled off her backpack and struggled with the contents before pulling out a small flashlight. "Not anymore!"

Panzer and Hernándo were hard at work clearing the jungle away from the circle of stelae. Panzer, kneeling, was chopping away at some vines that smothered the small limestone block. He had not noticed Woodson, Pedro and Lyons coming toward him until he saw their shadows fall on the stele he was uncovering. He turned to see who owned the shadows. Panzer knew immediately that something was wrong. He stood up and casually brushed off the debris that had collected on his clothes.

"Jon, we need to talk to you," said Woody.

"Sure, Woody, what's up? You guys look like you've lost your best friend."

"It's about this site…" Woodson began, but paused, hoping to find the right words to tell Panzer. Lyons wasted no time finishing the sentence for him.

"It's not Site Q.," he blurted.

"Nice going, Professor," growled Woodson. "A little tact isn't a bad thing,"

"He's a grown man. He can take it," snapped Lyons.

"I was about to tell him. Did you have to do that? Don't you think that the man has feelings? You know he is paying for all—"

"Stop!" cried Panzer loudly.

Woodson and Lyons stopped arguing and faced Panzer like two children caught misbehaving on a playground.

"Good. Now that I have your attention, *what are you two talking about?"*

The floor of the cave proved very slippery, but Blue and Carla, though they struggled, were able to navigate safely down the dark twisting cavern. Blue's flashlight was up to the task, though the inky blackness of the cave at times quickly absorbed the light. The walls were equally as moist as the rocky ground, leaving very few options for anything to hold onto. Twice Carla slipped and fell, but luckily without injury. The deeper they descended into the dark tunnel, the more they felt the cave walls reverberate from the water exploding over the cliff's jagged rocks. Blue stopped and turned off the flashlight.

"What are you doing?" Carla cried out so Blue could hear over the roar rushing through the cave. "Are you crazy?"

"Look!" exclaimed Blue, pointing at the glimmer of light just ahead.

"There's light up there! Can you see it?"

Blue turned the flashlight back on and they resumed their descent. Within the distance of fifty feet, the opening came into full view. Walking to the gap, they found themselves looking at the backside of the waterfall. Stepping through the mouth of the cave, they found that the path ended at a ledge only a scant few feet from the cascading water as it fell into the pool below. The ledge went off in two directions, both pitched downward, and both appeared passable.

"Wow! I can't believe this!" exclaimed Carla. She took out her camera to get a shot of the water as it crashed all around them.

"This ledge will probably lead us away from the falls and down to the pool below." Blue glanced in both directions. "But, which way?"

"I think we should go to the right," said Carla, pulling the wet hair from her face.

"It's fifty-fifty! Let's give it a try."

Blue and Carla made their way carefully down the mist covered ledge. The rocky shelf was wide enough that falling off the edge was not a concern as long as they stayed on their feet. They had only walked a few feet when confronted with another tunnel. This one was a little wider than the one that they had just traveled down

"C'mon Carla, it's not very long, I can see the other opening from here."

Slowly they made their way through the second cave and out the opening. Blue and Carla were blinded temporarily by the bright sunlight as they emerged from the second cave and onto a small rocky path. This path definitely led down to the beautiful, blue-green pool of water below.

"Eureka!" cried Blue. Then, with that beautiful pool in sight, a voice growled, its owner hidden by the jagged rocks above.

"*Good afternoon ladies.*" said the voice coldly.

Blue glanced up. Shading her eyes from the bright sun to get a better look, she could just make out the shadowy figure of a man against the bright sunlight. There was one thing that she was sure. Whoever it was held something metal that reflected like a mirror against the sun's bright glare. There was no mistake, it was a gun, and pointed right at them. Blue struggled to block the sun from her vision. She could barely see their assailants face but there was no doubt in her mind as to who it was.

"*Smith!*" she gasped.

CHAPTER NINETEEN
Capture and Escape

Blue stepped back; she was not certain what to do or how many men Smith had with him. Carla had the gun, but neither of them knew how to use it. Blue crept back a little further, finally bumping into Carla.

"What are we gonna do?" Carla whispered into Blue's ear.

"I'm not sure, but I do know that one of us has got to get away and bring help!"   Smith struggled down the rocks to the path. Blue watched him closely, desperately waiting for a chance to run as soon as he let his guard down. Suddenly that chance came! A rock under Smith's foot gave way, forcing him to turn away and grab something to keep from falling. Blue seized the moment.

"Back into the cave, *now!*" *s*he screamed. Blue pushed Carla toward the opening. The mouth of the cave was only a scant few feet behind them.

Suddenly, a gunshot and a ricochet as it hit the rocks above the cave entrance stopped them in their tracks. Blue grabbed Carla by the arm and looked her in the eyes. It was quite apparent to Blue how truly frightened Carla was. Her companion's eyes were as big as saucers.

"Go! Get back to camp and bring help," cried Blue

Carla gasped, "What about you?"

"Don't worry about me! I've handled tougher guys than this, *Go!*" Blue pushed Carla into the dark cave opening, nearly falling from the force she exerted. She turned to the sound of footsteps running up the path. Blue jumped up to face the gunman. It *was* Smith and he was running right toward her. There was a second man running some twenty feet down the path behind Smith, but he was of little concern. Blue held the flashlight up in the air like a club and braced herself for the attack.

Carla never looked back. She scrambled wildly across the ledge that ran behind the waterfall. She searched for the opening of the cave that would lead to safety and rescue. Carla shuddered at the thought of climbing up the cave with nothing to light her way, but that did not matter. All that mattered was getting to Woodson and the others for help— *she had to save Blue.*

Smith stopped a few feet short of Blue and the mouth of the cave. He was aware that Carla had escaped. He shot Blue an ugly smile.

"Are you planning on hitting me with that flashlight?" he asked calmly.

Blue held her ground. She was determined to keep Smith from catching Carla. "She got away, Smith. You can't catch her now!" she yelled in triumph. "Soon, my friends will be here to save me! So, you might as well let me go, too!" she warned still waving the flashlight over her head.

"Tsk, tsk, tsk." Smith shook his head. "That is exactly what I want," he snarled. "I *want* them to come to rescue you!" Smith paused for effect. "It will be much easier to kill your friends as they march one by one out of that tunnel, don't you think?"

A raging fury swelled up inside Blue. She lunged at Smith, swinging the flashlight wildly as she did. Smith quickly dodged the blow and grabbed Blue by the wrist. His grip felt like an iron vise. Smith snatched the flashlight from Blue's hand before throwing her to the ground.

"Nice try!" he said with a smirk. Smith turned to his companion. "I think we'd better tie this one up, Franz. She's quite the wildcat."

Carla felt her way carefully up the wet blackness of the cave. The walls felt even more slimy and slippery in the total darkness. The rocks beneath her feet were not much better. Carla knew that if she just kept going, she would reach the path and freedom. The thought that they might try to follow her continually crossed Carla's mind, but there was no sign of a light coming up the cave behind her. She knew they would not chase her in the dark, at least she hoped that they would not.

The smell of the damp cave filled her nostrils. She thought about how odd it was that she did not notice the musty, damp smell before. The scrapes and scratches on her hands stung from rubbing against the rocky cave wall.

As she made it further up the cave, the walls felt dryer. Even the footing improved. Carla knew that the opening of the cave had to be just ahead.

Then, as if she had willed it, there it was. The entrance to the cave was just ahead. In a few moments, she would be on her way back to camp. Exploding into the bright afternoon sunlight, she paused for a very brief moment to catch her breath.

"Do you think that Woody and my friends are just going to stand there and let you kill them?" growled Blue. Franz tightened the rope around her wrists. "You're gonna *wish* you were dead after Woody gets finished with you!"

"It ends today, my dear. I have too much time and money invested in this little scam to just walk away and let *you* people turn it into another tourist trap!" Smith replied.

"Scam! What are you talking about, Smith?" Blue winced as Franz pulled the rope tighter.

"I'm sure your friend, Woodson, would have figured it out by now."

"Figured what out?"

"That this is not Site Q. There is no Site Q!"

"What about the stelae you've been selling on the black market?"

"The collectors are so eager for new artifacts that they will believe anything. Site Q. is a legend in the archeological world. That makes anything that might come from it very, very valuable. There is not one Site Q., there are Site Q's everywhere the chicleros find them. At least until *you* people come around!" Smith paused for a moment to double check the ropes around Blue's wrists. "Good job Franz, that ought to hold her for a little while!"

Blue suddenly remembered the other day when Woodson had her read what he had translated from the pottery shard. She remembered sensing that Woodson saw something on that codex pottery that disturbed him. *He knows*, she thought.

"I can't believe that you would kill us all to keep this place a secret," she said in disbelief.

"You weren't even supposed to find this site," snapped Smith. "If my man had done his job like he was supposed to, you people would either already be dead or at least hopelessly lost!"

"You mean Hernándo!" she laughed. "Woody had his number right away. Your goon didn't fool him for a minute!"

"Interesting," Smith replied thoughtfully. "I am curious as to why my orders haven't been carried out. I'll have to ask Hernándo after we've taken care of you and your friends."

"Woody will take care of *you, and* Hernándo *and* your funny looking friend here. So you'd better let me go!" warned Blue.

"No my dear, the hunter never lets the bait go free."

Carla burst from the jungle onto the path that led back to camp. Everything was happening in slow motion; it seemed to be taking her forever to reach the camp. Carla was exhausted, her sides ached, and she could barely catch her breath, but she pushed herself on. It was Blue's only chance. Up ahead, she spotted Woodson and Lyons standing near the path. Her lungs ached and her mouth was dry, but she managed a muted scream.

"Help!" she cried. Woodson rushed toward her, Lyons right behind.

"What's wrong?" asked Lyons, once they had reached Carla.

Carla fell at their feet. She was out of breath and completely exhausted. Mustering up all her strength, she sat up and pointed down the path.

"Where's Blue?" asked Woodson, looking down the path in the direction that Carla had just come.

"Blue!" her voice cracked, a raspy whisper. "Smith has her!"

"What?" cried Woodson. He and Lyons helped Carla to her feet. "What are you talking about?"

Carla still labored to catch her breath. "The waterfall, Woody, he has her at the waterfall!"

"Can you take us to her?"

"Yes... I can." Carla collapsed into Lyons' arms.

"Carla, Carla!" pleaded Woodson, but it was useless, Carla was out cold.

Lyons laid her down on the path. Pedro appeared with a canteen and a handkerchief.

"She isn't going anywhere, Woody. I think she's in some kind of shock!" Lyons exclaimed. Pedro soaked a handkerchief and gently wet her lips.

"I need her! It could take hours for us to find that waterfall. Blue could be dead by then!"

"Sorry Woody, she could be out for awhile."

Woodson paced frantically, Pedro and Keh tried to calm him, but to no avail.

"I guess I have no choice. I'm going after Blue! Pedro, I want you and Keh to come with me. Hernándo, you stay here with Lyons and Panzer. Keep an eye out for chicleros. Bending down over Carla, he removed the gun from her belt. Slipping it to Lyons, he whispered, "If Hernándo even looks at either of you funny, *shoot him!*"

"Pedro, I'll need my bow. I think we'd better go back to camp before we—"

Hernándo grabbed Woodson by his shoulder and turned him around. "I know the way," he said calmly. "I will show you."

Woodson looked deep into the large Mayan's eyes and asked, "Why?"

"I owe you and the old one my life. If you want to save the woman, you must hurry. Smith is capable of anything."

CHAPTER TWENTY
The Final Confrontation

"Professor, I want you and Panzer to stay close to camp. Keep an eye out for chicleros. I think there were only two of them, but you never can tell... Keh! Where's Keh?" asked Woodson as he strung his bow.

Pedro stepped out of Keh's tent and motioned to Woodson. Quickly, Woodson ducked through the opening to find the dark figure of Keh kneeling on his mat, chanting over a small pot of burning incense. As his eyes became more accustomed to the dimly lit tent, Woodson noticed the shaman held a small knife directly over the acrid smoke.

"I want you to stay here just in case Smith has chicleros with him. Lyons could use your help."

"No! I go with you!" replied Keh.

Look, I do *not* have time to argue with you. I need you here."

No! I will go with you! The spirits—your nawal say I must help to protect you and the boy."

Keh stood and carefully tucked the knife into the sash, before tying a red band around his head, just above the eyes.

"Well Professor, if we must, it *is* a good day to die," he continued. He walked to the tent opening and held the flap open for Woodson.

"Nobody's going to die today—except maybe Smith," growled Woodson. "If he's harmed one hair on Blue's head, I swear I'll kill him myself!" Woodson squeezed his bow so tightly that his knuckles turned white.

Keh grabbed Woodson's arm. The old man's grip was firm, like steel.

"It is time for us to save your woman."

The day had given way to the long shadows of the late afternoon. Blue sat on a large rock, just off the path, near the waterfall. She felt tired and both of her wrists burned from trying to loosen the rope. Smith and Franz rested only a few feet from her, each perched on his own rock.

"What does a girl gotta do to get a drink of water around here?" she asked sarcastically, in a parched raspy voice, "I'm thirsty!"

Franz stood and glared at the helpless captive.

"If you don't shut up, you'll find out what a girl's got to do for a drink of water!" he warned, holding a menacing fist to Blue's face.

Blue spit on his fist.

"If you even touch me, Woody will kill you! Both of you!" she exclaimed, just before Franz slapped her across the face. The blow knocked Blue off her rock. She rolled painfully onto the path.

Smith jumped to his feet. "Franz, that's enough!"

"Why don't we just kill her and ambush her friends before they get here? Why do we need all the dramatics?"

"We have the advantage here, Franz," replied Smith calmly. "They have to come down this path and we'll be waiting for them." He waved his gun in the direction of the cave opening that led to the waterfall. "Should we be so sloppy as to miss them as they come charging out of that tunnel, our large Mayan friend will make sure they don't run away." Smith helped Blue up onto her feet. He gave her a sip from his canteen. "You see Franz, this is the way you treat a guest. Especially when this is their last day on earth."

Franz was beginning to demonstrate his frustration.

"Why not just throw her over the falls and be done with it?"

Smith grabbed Franz roughly by the arm and growled, "Because, you idiot, if Woodson thinks that we've killed her, he will come after us in a blind rage. If he knows that she is still alive—and we will let him *see* that she is still alive—he will be careful not to hurt our little guest here. *Do you understand?*"

Franz attempted to pull away from Smith's strong hold, but could not break free. Smith smirked and released his grip. Franz shook his head and walked away, mumbling. Smith then turned his attention to Blue.

"There! You're safe my dear, for now!"

Hernándo led the way as the group struggled down the misty cavern. Pedro and Woodson followed close behind. Woodson was still uncertain of Hernándo's loyalty, but realized that at this point, they had no choice. Pedro was right behind the large Maya, flashlight in hand, watching his every move.

Keh had slipped twice falling down onto the moist rocky surface. Uninjured by the falls, the old shaman urged the group to go ahead insisting that he would soon catch them. Woodson was concerned about the old man's safety, but right now, Blues' life was at stake and that had to be the priority.

"Go ahead!" the old shaman had protested. "The spirits will lead me to you when the time is right. *Now go!*"

"How much farther?" Woodson called out to the guide.

"Soon, Professor, you can hear the waterfall," replied the Mayan.

Woodson could hear the rushing of the falls. It seemed to grow louder with every step. Hernándo switched off his flashlight.

"Turn off your lights," cried Hernándo.

Cautiously, Woodson and Pedro complied.

"Look!"

Woodson thought he saw a dim light ahead. It must have been the opening to the other end of the cave.

"Yes, I see light ahead. Let's get going."

Hernándo turned around; his enormous frame blocked the narrow path.

"No!" he exclaimed.

Woodson threw his weight against Hernándo to push him out of the way. It was no use—the guide was too strong. "I knew you couldn't be trusted!" Woodson tried once more to move Hernándo, but the Mayan's great strength was much more than a match for his own. Even with Pedro's help, they could not move his large body enough to get by. Hernándo grabbed them both by the arm.

"Listen to me!" he cried, easily holding Woodson and Pedro in check. "You must trust me, Professor," he said, releasing his grip. "Because of the noise from falls, we will not be able to hear each other without speaking loudly. The tunnel will carry our voices. Smith will know that we come." Hernándo shook his head. "It is important that I tell you now what we need to do. Once we go out that end of the tunnel, we will be right behind the falls. Believe me when I tell you that you will not be able to hear me!" Hernándo paused and placed a large hand on both Woodson and Pedro's shoulder. With a firm grip, he pulled them in as close as he could.

"This is what we must do…"

"Carla? Are you feeling better?" whispered Lyons. The professor knelt by her side. "Are you sure you wouldn't feel better inside your tent, my dear?"

"No Professor, I'm feeling much better and the fresh air feels good," she replied. Carla reached out and touched his hand. She appeared tired and pale but her voice was beginning to sound a little stronger. "What about Blue? Is she okay?"

Lyons shook his head slowly, "I'm afraid that I cannot answer that. Woody and the others left some time ago. I'm beginning to get a little worried, myself."

Carla gave his hand a gentle, affectionate squeeze and replied softly, "I'm sure they will find her and take care of that snake—" Carla's concerned expression suddenly turned to fear. Letting go of his hand she raised her arm and pointed over Lyon's shoulder. Her hand was shaking. *"Look out!"* she screamed.

Lyons turned to look just in time. A smallish man, dressed in white was coming straight at him—the man's arm over his head. Lyon's gaze followed the man's arm up to his hand. The intruder was holding a deadly machete and was preparing to strike. Lyons reached for his gun, but knew there was not enough time to fire off a round. He prepared himself for the blow when, from out of nowhere, a body flew at his assailant knocking him to the ground.

"Panzer!" exclaimed Lyons. He rushed to Panzer's aid.

Panzer and the assailant were locked in a desperate struggle for the machete. Lyons was just about to pull the attacker off when Panzer screamed, *"Professor, behind you!"*

Lyons turned to meet the second attacker. The chiclero was nearly on the professor when Lyons took aim and fired his pistol at point blank range. The attacker stopped instantly before slowly slumping to the ground.

Upon hearing the gunshot, the first chiclero stopped struggling with Panzer.

"No!" he screamed in anguish. The chiclero pushed Panzer away, struggled to his feet and jumped at Lyons. Another shot rang out. This time over the attackers head, stopping him instantly. Lyons pointed the pistol right at the

chicleros heart. He was at point blank range. There was no way that Lyons could miss and the chiclero knew it.

"Drop the machete," demanded the professor, waving the pistol toward the ground. *"Now!"*

The sound of the water as it plummeted onto the rocks below was deafening. The ledge that ran behind the falls was slippery, but more than wide enough as Hernándo led the way out of the tunnel. Woodson held his bow and quiver as far away from the falling water as he could. A slippery bowstring or arrow could cost him precious seconds.

As Hernándo had planned, Woodson took the lead as they headed down the ledge toward the opening. Pedro and Keh brought up the rear. They were to stay out of sight until the time was right.

Woodson felt his way through the last part of the cave, until the sunlight that entered the opening was sufficient to light the way. After he traveled a few more feet, he noticed that the path led down the rocks, probably to the pool below. Just as Woodson reached the opening, he looked back at the large Mayan. Hernándo smiled and nodded for him to proceed.

Woodson thought, *I can't believe that I trust this character. What am I doing?* As he stepped out of the tunnel and onto the path, he realized that it was too late to worry about trust or anything else for that matter. Smith was right there in front of him, and he had Blue. The muzzle of Smith's gun pointed directly at her head.

"Welcome to the party, Professor," Smith said, grinning widely. Woodson started toward them, but Hernándo grabbed him from behind. He stopped quickly, anticipating the large Mayan's iron grip to tighten around his arms.

Betrayed, he thought, *I should have known!* Woodson began to struggle.

"Let her go, Smith! You can't get away with this!"

"I can and I will, Professor. *Oh, I will!*"

"What do you plan to do with us?"

"Kill you, of course. I can't have you turning this place into another tourist trap, very bad for business.

"What business?" growled Woodson. "Stealing national treasures from the people? You are depriving generations of children from learning more about one of the most fascinating ancient cultures that has ever existed!"

"Maybe, but the collectors pay big bucks for these antiquities and it sure beats working for a living. Right, Franz?" Smith smirked and looked in the direction of the small sailor.

"You can't get away with this, Smith, so you can wipe that silly look off your face," snapped Woodson. "My friends will tell the authorities and you'll get caught, no matter what happens to us!"

"Oh! That's right, your friend Panzer and the esteemed Professor Lyons."

"It's too late. I told them to wait for only so long before getting out of there. You won't get them!" Woodson exclaimed loudly, his voice filled with rage.

"I believe you're right. It is too late, Professor Woodson. My chicleros have probably killed them already."

With all of his strength, Woodson attempted to break away from Hernándo. His body shook, straining to get loose. He wanted to get his hands on Smith so badly he could taste it. Slowly, Hernándo released his grip on Woodson's straining arm. He was free! Woodson started toward Smith, but stopped when he heard the sound of Smith pulling back the hammer of the gun. There was no question in Woodson's mind. Smith *was* crazy enough to pull the trigger.

"That's better, Professor. I didn't think you wanted to watch me blow your girlfriend's brains out."

Woodson fought to gain control of his rage. Regaining his composure, he turned his attention to Blue.

"Blue! Are you okay?"

"Do I look okay to you?" she asked sarcastically.

"How do you do it? You find trouble wherever we go," said Woodson.

"I suppose this is my fault?"

"What do you think? It wasn't my idea for you to go running off—"

"Enough!" screamed Smith angrily. "Could you two please stop arguing? I'm getting a headache." Smith waved the gun playfully at Woodson. "Now drop the bow and arrows." Woodson let the weapons fall gently to the ground. Immediately, Hernándo kicked them away then regained his iron grip on Woodson's arms "Now, my large friend, would you please take our guest over to the edge of the cliff?"

Woodson strained to pull away from Hernándo.

"If you harm one hair on her head, I swear, I'll kill you with my bare hands—*all of you!"* he growled, teeth clenched in rage.

"Kill them already, Smith! This is getting tiresome," yelled Franz.

"When I'm good and ready," Smith growled.

Pedro pulled Keh back away from the cave opening. Certain that they had not been seen by Smith, he wondered if Hernándo had betrayed them. At this point, neither he nor Woodson were sure of his intentions. What was happening was not according to the plan. Hernándo was supposed to pretend to restrain his friend, but from the way Woodson was struggling, Pedro knew that something had to be wrong. Carefully, he peered out the opening. Woodson and Blue were in plain sight, but because of the noise from the falls, he could not hear a thing. All that Pedro and Keh could do was stay out of sight and hope.

The young chiclero dropped his machete and moved toward the body of his fallen comrade.

"Alto!" Lyons yelled. He aimed his pistol at the young man's face. *"Stop right where you are, Señor!"*

The young man looked at Lyons and motioned toward the lifeless body. Carla struggled to her knees and called out to Lyons, "I think he just wants to help the other man!"

With a sigh, Lyons slowly dropped the barrel of his gun and motioned to the chiclero to attend to his friend.

"Panzer, you all right?" he asked. Jon stood and brushed himself off.

"Just a couple of scratches, that's all," he replied. His voice sounded a little shaky.

Lyons looked at Panzer again just to make certain. Panzer's shoulder was bleeding badly. Lyons rushed to his side, while still keeping a watchful eye on the chiclero.

"I think you'd better sit down, old man. That shoulder looks like it might be cut pretty bad." With that, Panzer gently touched the shoulder with his other hand. As soon as Panzer saw the blood, he passed out cold into Lyons' arms.

Carla quickly got to her feet.

"Professor, can I help?" she asked in a weakened, hoarse voice.

Lyons looked up, "Are you strong enough, my dear?" he asked. Carla nodded slowly and smiled. "Here, take the gun and keep an eye on those two over there!"

Carla took the gun and turned toward the chicleros and said, "I don't think that will be necessary, Professor. Look!"

Lyons turned to see the younger man holding the fallen man in his arms. He was crying. His sobs conveyed that the other man was very important to him. By the sound of the young man's sorrow, the older man must have been badly hurt, or dead.

CHAPTER TWENTY-ONE
In Search of Site Q.

Woodson heard the roar of the water crashing against the rocks below. He spied the calm pool of water where Blue and Carla had planned to bathe. *How calm and tranquil*, he thought, *in the midst of all the power of the raging falls.* Hernándo had pushed him up to the edge of the cliff. Woodson felt the rocks beneath his feet begin to give way. He tried desperately to maintain his balance. One false move and he was over the edge.

"Pretty isn't it?" Smith asked sarcastically, "Looks almost inviting. I think he could do with a little swim. What do you think, Hernándo? It is a pity that there are so many rocks in the way. My guess is that you will probably be quite dead by the time you hit the water." Smith sneered, as he pulled Blue closer to the edge. "Watch closely. *You're next!*"

"No!" she cried. *"You can't!"*

Smith tightened his grip on Blue and yelled to the large Mayan, "Now, Hernándo! Throw him over the side!"

Woodson become rigid, he was prepared to die, but not without a fight. Just as he began to struggle, Woodson felt Hernándo let go his grip.

"No, Smith. I owe this man my life. I cannot take his." Hernándo stated calmly. "If you want this man dead you will have to kill him yourself."

Smith glared at Hernándo in disbelief.

"Okay," he said brightly, then raised his pistol and shot Woodson.

"Woody!" cried Blue. Woodson spun around and slumped to the ground.

Suddenly, the wind began to howl and cry. The sky quickly filled with dark, ominous clouds. A swirling mist fell from the sky. Hidden in the cave, Keh felt a presence—the *nawal* were all around them. He knew it!

"We must help them, Pedro," he cried. "Somehow we must!"

"I know, but how?" Pedro replied. "We have no weapon."

Keh looked out onto the path. He grabbed Pedro and pointed down toward the ground.

"Yes, we do, my son!" he exclaimed.

The howling wind swirled bitterly as Blue stared at her fallen love. A maddening rage began to build inside her. Turning her head, she looked her captor menacingly in the eye. Smith, taken back by the madness in her eyes and the loud howling winds that surrounded him, released his grip. She was free.

In an instant of blind rage, she lowered her head and lunged at Smith. Not expecting her attack, he fell back, nearly falling over the edge. Franz jumped up and grabbed Blue from behind. She felt his fingers dig deeply into the flesh of her upper arm. "Aarrrgh!" she growled in pain.

Suddenly, something whistled past her head. Franz's grip suddenly disappeared. Blue turned her attention back to Smith, his face looked contorted as if he were in shock.

"I've been shot!" screamed Franz, Blue turned back to see Franz holding his shoulder. There was blood everywhere. The wounded man fell to his knees. Now she knew why Smith looked so shocked.

Hernándo grabbed her and threw her out of the way. Now lying on the ground, Blue could clearly see what had happened to Franz. The long, black shaft of an arrow protruded from his back. It had passed all the way through his shoulder. Looking beyond the wounded man, she watched as Woodson struggled to his knees.

Hernándo rushed wildly toward Smith. They began to struggle, but Smith was no match for Hernándo's great strength. The Mayan grabbed him, and with both hands, lifted Smith over his head. The sight of this enormous man holding Smith up to the darkening sky was frightening. Woodson knew what was about to happen, his *nawal* was causing Hernándo to act violently. He also knew that he could do nothing about it, but he had to try.

"No, Hernándo! Stop!" warned Woodson. *"Don't do it!"*

Woodson was up on his feet. Holding his wounded shoulder, he lunged toward Hernándo. Pedro rushed to help Woodson.

"No, Hernándo! No!" pleaded Smith, but he knew that it was too late. Then in an instant, Hernándo threw the smuggler to the ground near the edge of the cliff just out of sight. Woodson and Pedro were both certain that the villain had plunged to his death onto the jagged rocks below. Then, they heard a soft whimper come from just beyond a large rock.

"Don't let him kill me, Woodson," cried the voice. It was Smith. He was still alive! Woodson and Pedro rushed to the edge and pulled Smith to his feet. "The Mayan is crazy," he snapped. "Keep him away from me!"

Woodson laughed, "You know Smith, I'm really going to enjoy handing you over to the police."

"I'll go! I'll go!" replied Smith excitedly. "Just keep him away from me!"

Hernándo placed his hand on Woodson's wounded shoulder.

"Now we are even, Professor! You have saved my life, now I have saved yours." He turned toward Keh, who was helping Blue to her feet. "But, I still owe you, old man!"

Keh untied Blue's wrists. She ran to Woodson throwing her arms wildly around his neck.

"We are even as well, my son," replied Keh. "He would have undoubtedly killed me too!"

"Then it is finished," said Hernándo. He pulled the wounded Franz to his feet, "except for this one. What do you want me to do with him?"

Woodson bent over to check Franz's wound.

"He's no worse off than I am," he said. "Let's get that arrow out of him and see if we can stop the bleeding."

"Are you sure that *you're* okay?" Pedro asked nervously upon seeing his mentor's wound.

Woodson looked at his bow that Pedro firmly gripped in his hand.

"Where did you learn to shoot like that, Pedro?" he asked with a smile.

"I think another's hand guided that arrow, Woody!" said Pedro. The young man handed his good friend the bow. Woodson smiled and squeezed Pedro's shoulder.

Woodson walked back to the edge of the cliff and gazed down in silence. The wind had stopped and the air smelled clean and fresh. He had experienced this smell before. Once at the caves when he met Keh and once in the old man's tent. He knew that everything would be okay. Woodson felt it deep within.

Keh now stood by his side. Together, they looked into the eyes of Woodson's *nawal*. In the pool of blue water below, Woodson could swear he saw the face of a woman. He looked at Keh. The old man just smiled back and said, "Yes my son, Zazhal ab!"

Woodson looked into the pool again. This time he thought that he had seen another face in the still, shining water, a man's face. He looked at Keh again. Keh smiled and pointed at Pedro.

"You mean..."

"Yes, my son," replied Keh happily. "It seems that your young friend has someone who watches over him as well."

"The arrow," whispered Woodson.

Keh nodded, a gleam of great satisfaction filled his old, wise eyes.

Woodson knew what the shaman meant. All along, he thought that the spirit that haunted his dreams was Guerrero. Now, he knew differently. He and Pedro were blessed, blessed with the spirits of old who protected them. Woodson now knew his spirit. He hoped that someday Pedro would know his as well.

Woodson pulled Guerrero's green beads from his pocket. He brought them up to his lips and kissed them. Without a word, he threw them into the shimmering, blue pool below.

"That's why I could see Guerrero die in my visions, isn't it Keh?" he asked. Woodson watched the beads hit rock after rock before finally coming to rest in the calm pool below.

"That is correct."

"How long have you known?"

"From the moment we met."

"The spirits brought us here to save the ruins from looters."

Keh nodded. Nothing more needed to be said. The spirits had done their job. The ruins were safe.

"What about the small village?" asked Woodson. "What about those spirits?"

Keh smiled and said, "Maybe that should be left for another adventure. I think we have all had enough excitement, don't you?"

Woodson laughed. "Yeah, maybe you're right."

Blue looked into Woodson's eyes.

"Are you all right, Woody?" she asked. Woodson just looked at her and smiled.

"He is fine, Blue," replied Keh. The old shaman dropped to his knees chanting happily to the spirit of Zazhal ab. He wanted to give the spirits a proper sendoff to the underworld and finally peace.

Back in El Naranjo Woodson and Blue stood talking in the square. They were waiting for the bus that would take them back to Santa Elena.

"Woody, are you sure everything is all right?" she asked. Blue pushed her windblown hair from her eyes,

"Everything is fine, really. Now that I know who has been haunting me for so many years, I can get on with my life—our life."

"So, are we going back to Chicago?"

"Nope, Cozumel. Angel and I have a lot to talk about. I'm still on leave from the University and Panzer paid us pretty well—so why not?"

"Sounds good to me, Woody, though, I'm going to miss everyone. I wish Pedro and the professor was coming with us."

"Me too, but Pedro and Keh are going to stay with Panzer and Hernándo to continue the search for Site Q. Maybe it *is* out there. On the other hand, maybe Smith was right. Who knows?"

"If it's there, I'll find it!" exclaimed Pedro.

"You just be careful."

"I will keep an eye on him, Woody," said Keh.

"How come everybody has to keep an eye on me?" Pedro began to protest.

Woodson shook his head, "You just do as Keh says. Got it!"

"Okay," replied Pedro.

"I think it's great that Lyons and Carla are going to stay down here and supervise the restoration of the lost city," said Blue. "You know, Woody, I kind of thought that you were sweet on Carla there for awhile."

Woodson paused and looked deeply into Blue's eyes.

"You know Blue; you never did tell me what you were doing in Playa del Carmen when we were chasing after that codex."

"What do you think, you big dope? That I ran into you by accident. I had been at the ruins at Coba doing some research. Pedro knew it, but I didn't want you to. I was going to surprise you at Tulum. Then, everything went up for grabs. Pedro left word that you were headed for the Playa and the rest is history."

"I should have known. You couldn't live without me!"

"Oh, I *could* live without you! I just thought it would be more fun to live *with* you."

"Is this where I'm supposed to take you up in my arms and give you a romantic kiss?"

"No more kissing!" cried Pedro just before Keh grabbed the boy's ear and pulled him away.

"That would be a good start," replied Blue, putting her arms around Woodson.

So, he did.

The End

Pumpkinhead Productions
Please visit us on Facebook

If you enjoyed this title, you may enjoy reading The Fifth Codex. Take an action packed trip into the mysterious world of the Maya.

At Tulum, a Mayan archeological site in the Yucatan peninsula, Richard Woodson, a well-known archeologist, and his sixteen-year-old apprentice, Pedro a native Mayan, find a journal hidden in the ruins for hundreds of years— a journal written by Gonzalo Guerrero the first Spaniard to live among the Maya. As Pedro and Woodson translate the document, they realize that Guerrero had stumbled onto something that he could not have possibly understood. At first, the mystery appeared to be the existence of an ancient lost city. What Woodson and Pedro discovered was the existence of a rare codex (book)—The Fifth Codex—and set out to find it!

About the Author

Robert Bresloff is a novelist specializing in juvenile and middle school age adventure books. His first two novels in the "Bound into the Classics" series, originally published by Gauthier Publications for their now defunct Hungry Goat Press, *The Wee Musketeers,* and *Robin and the Little Hoods* are part of the Sylvan Book Adventure. Recently, Pumpkinhead Productions released Robert's third novel in the series, *The Wiz Kids of Oz. The Fifth Codex* is the first novel in Robert Bresloff's Pumpkinhead Productions three part "Mayan Adventure" series. His previous titles for Pumpkinhead Productions include *Cahokia: Mystery of Monks Mound* (2012) Robert will appear in the 2013 issue of Gale Publishing's Something About the Author (SATA) Recently Strict Publishing International released Scalawag and in November, Strict released his newest novel, *Pirates Alley.*

Printed in Great Britain
by Amazon.co.uk, Ltd.,
Marston Gate.